THE PROMISE OF THE COPPER SCROLL

ALAN MOSS

This is a work of fiction. Names, characters, places, and incidents are products of the author's imagination or are used fictitiously and are not to be construed as real. Any resemblance to actual events, locations, organizations, or persons, living or dead, is entirely coincidental.

World Castle Publishing, LLC

Pensacola, Florida
Copyright © 2024 Alan Moss
Hardback ISBN: 9798333083418
Paperback ISBN: 9798891262485
eBook ISBN: 9798891262492
First Edition World Castle Publishing, LLC, July 29, 2024
http://www.worldcastlepublishing.com

Licensing Notes

Cover: Cover Designs by Karen
Cover-designs-by-karen.com
Editor: Karen Fuller

A special thank you to Kelly Abell
for her insight and encouragement.
FOR THS 61

PROLOGUE
THURSDAY, APRIL 12, 1981
PETRA, JORDAN

Despite it being an early hour of the day, the temperature held at ninety-two degrees. Sam Wadsworth, a student of the antiquities, stood outside the Town Bazaar antique shop in Petra, Jordan. Petra was the center of the Arab kingdom in Hellenistic and Roman times.

Sitting in the middle of a severe desert, the miracle of Petra was an underground water system that transported spring water from the mountains five miles away. With that resource in hand, Petra's residents were able to construct a great stone temple and other buildings that have stood the test of time.

Wadsworth brightened as the proprietor raised the shade on the inside of the front door. Middle age with a grey beard, he spent an excessive amount of time looking outside. Then, he opened the door slowly, staring at the student, his first customer of the day.

A sign to the side of the door assured customers that English and French were spoken, as well as Arabic.

"Yes, come in. What may I show you?"

Not fully prepared to explain his task, Sam hesitated.

The proprietor had little patience.

"I'm a busy man. You need to explain your presence here or come again another day."

Wadsworth persevered.

"Well, sir, I am a seminary student back in the United States, in Princeton. I have studied Petra, how its underground system transported water from the mountains. I am wondering if anyone has recovered and preserved a sample of the ceramic pipes that carried the water."

A new respect was infused into the store owner.

"And what would be the purpose of finding such a pipe?"

"Well, given the temperature extremes between the water and the desert environment and the requirement that pipe sections would have to be leak-proof, I thought it might be useful to analyze such pipe and describe its content and characteristics. Today, there are manufacturers of ceramic pipe that are used in wastewater systems."

"This might make a useful research project," the proprietor responded. "Unfortunately, when diggers unearth sections of our ancient water system, they find that the pipe has worn away, leaving bare rock behind."

"Might the remaining rock contain elements from the ceramic pipe?" Wadsworth asked.

"That, my boy, would be a question for those who study underground rock formations. So, unless you are in the market for some of the rare antiques in my shop, peace be with you."

The student thanked the store owner for the information and headed toward Al-Arabi Restaurant, he passed on his way to the antique shop.

He turned to take a last look at the store and spotted three youths walking towards the location. They were carrying something under their loosely fitting black jackets.

The student decided to hold his place and see if there was trouble brewing.

Before he entered the seminary, Wadsworth worked with guidance counselors combatting inner city youth violence. There was something about the young people approaching the store that reminded him of that challenge. He turned towards the store, preparing to intervene if necessary.

The three hoods pulled metal rods from under their clothing. The proprietor spotted them and tried to lock the door. There was unmistakable fear in his eyes.

The door was pushed open, and one of the hoods swung his rod at the shop owner, grazing his left shoulder. The two remaining delinquents held the proprietor's arms, allowing the third to have a clear shot at him.

So involved with the shopkeeper, they left the door wide open and did not see a fast- approaching figure. Wadsworth, a Purple Belt – 3rd KYU, removed the rod from the attacking youth and chopped his neck, leaving him unconscious. With no delay, he spun around, disabling the legs of the other two, each falling to the floor in excruciating pain.

With the three intruders now tied securely to one another on the floor behind the counter and the proprietor recovered enough to speak, he called the Desert Police and reported the assault. With sincere gratitude, he addressed the seminary student:

"I cannot thank you enough. These ruffians have been terrorizing many shopkeepers, blackmailing them to pay for protection or be beaten. You sent a message that should end their threats. The police will question them, find out who is behind this scheme, and send them away for a long time.

"I promise, when the time is right, I will repay you for your kindness and quick action."

PART ONE
SEEING THE FUTURE

CHAPTER 1
WEDNESDAY, JULY 17, 2019
PRINCETON, NEW JERSEY

The distinguished Special Programs Director of the Princeton Public Library stood at the head of a capacity crowd in the ground level, glass enclosed lecture hall. She would introduce an unusual speaker.

"As most of you know, Princeton is a historic New Jersey town featuring an Ivy League university. The brilliant staff and student body there are dedicated to the advancement of knowledge in fields from political science to civil engineering.

"Here at the Princeton Public Library, we also pursue our town's thirst for knowledge. Founded in 1909, visitors borrow 550,000 items per year. More than the basic services, the institution offers numerous special programs, from an annual children's book festival to a three-part lecture series on the Vietnam War.

"Today, the topic is terrorism, and the speaker is Joan MacLennan, Regional Director of the Federal Bureau of Investigations."

Waiting to be introduced, Joan sat in one of three chairs at the head of the hall, facing the audience. An attractive woman, she was in her thirties, having moved-up at a rapid pace. Her promotions reflected an uncanny ability to analyze indications of terrorist activity and act to prevent the loss of life.

While she was confident in her investigative skills, being a public figure, explaining the fundamentals of terrorism, and responding to audience questions and comments was something new. But, her supervisor insisted that she utilize her knowledge to help inform the public about the dangers of terrorist activities.

Earlier that morning, at 4:00 am, she received a tip from an informant with a reliable record. He claimed that a man in a North Philadelphia neighborhood was organizing a mass robbery that would overwhelm salespeople at a fine jewelry store in a popular downtown location. What made the tip even more urgent was the allegation that the leader had acquired an assault weapon.

Her instincts told her to act. Hoping to prevent the threatened violence, she ordered local, state, and FBI resources to the area.

After a generous introduction, she rose and

made her way to the microphone, appreciating the audience's applause. She delayed her address, as her mind couldn't stay away from the dangerous situation in *the city of brotherly love.*

With the audience becoming impatient, Joan forced herself to begin her speech.

"Thank you so much.

"This is a difficult topic to address in such a beautiful and peaceful community as Princeton. However, what we've learned, especially since the nine-eleven attacks in 2001, is that public awareness can play a significant role in preventing or minimizing terrorist activity. What if the instructors teaching Arab immigrants how to fly but not land airlines had alerted the FBI to their limited instruction agenda?

"Over the next hour, I will cover the history of terrorism, beginning with biblical times; the four types of terrorism; how terrorists provoke authorities into using illegal, unconstitutional, and repressive measures and thereby lose public support; and what you may do to understand foreign and domestic terrorist threats. Then, I will be glad to open the proceedings to your questions and comments."

After another round of applause following the Q&A session, the library staff said their thanks, and MacLennan was whisked away and back to her office in Trenton.

She was relieved to learn that the man with the assault weapon and his gang were taken into custody before they could do any damage. While this was a significant victory, the growing number of terrorist attacks would keep her in a constant state of tense awareness.

Nancy Troll sat through the lecture, enthusiastic about the information MacLennan provided. Nancy was a senior at nearby Drexel University. Her senior project involved the study of a copper scroll, rumored to provide directions to a biblical treasure. Her goal wasn't to find the gold, silver, and valuable temple ornaments covered by the scroll but to develop stories that could form the basis of a series of newspaper articles or even a TV special.

Experience gained writing for her high school newspaper, and then the Drexel Triangle convinced the young lady that being a reporter had to be her profession. She spent many hours late into the night determining story content and then writing it up for publication. The thrill of seeing her byline published fulfilled her professional desires.

As the crowd filed out, Nancy recognized Carol Stark, secretary-assistant to the Research Director of the nearby Princeton Seminary.

"Carol, did you attend for Director Wadsworth?"

"Hi Nancy, yes, he's overseas and asked

that I brief him on the presentation. What was your motivation?"

"Given my interest in the copper scroll and its Middle East origins, the more I know about terrorists and how they operate, the better. Antiquities appear to be a magnet for terrorism."

"That's right, we met when you asked me to set up your interview with the Director."

The two finally exited through the door to Witherspoon Street. Nancy turned to face Carol.

"I have my car. If you're going back to the Seminary, it's on my way."

"That would be great. Much faster than the bus."

As the two traveled the back roads of Princeton, Nancy explained how the goal of her senior project was to write articles about the copper scroll, the antiquity rumored to provide a path to the treasure hidden to avoid capture by the Roman army in the year 70 AD. Ignoring the highly competitive nature of newspaper and broadcast reporting, she went on to express confidence that upon graduation, her work might be recognized with a reporter job with a major newspaper or TV station.

As Nancy expressed youthful optimism about the future, Carol retreated in worry. While she had a husband she loved and two beautiful children, her husband's addiction to sports gambling destroyed the equity in their house and threatened their marriage. She had to find a way to turn things around.

Although she loved her husband, divorce appeared to be one practical way out. She had a good job at the Seminary. Without the burden of her husband's debt, she might be able to take care of the family on her own. On the other hand, divorce would break the close bonds on which she and the kids have relied.

Nancy's Honda pulled to a stop in front of the main Seminary building.

"I'm going to visit friends at the beach next week. Let's get together for coffee when I return."

"Sounds good," Carol responded as she exited the car and walked into the building.

CHAPTER 2

It was a beautiful summer night in Margate, a small beach community on the ocean. Nancy agreed to walk to Lamberti's, her favorite bar and restaurant. Open from May to October, the wood structure faced the bay. Because it was not open year-round, the service was often subpar. But the Italian-seafood cuisine was wonderful, and the drinks were potent. Most of the tables were under the stars providing a feeling of freedom and relaxation. Always the first to be ready, Nancy agreed to reserve a table for her and the three girlfriends she was visiting for the week.

She walked up three steps and approached the hostess in charge of reservations.

"Hi, Debbie. We need a table for four tonight."

With the restaurant crowded and many standing at the bar, Nancy wondered how long they would have to wait.

"Looks like we're talking about an hour or more."

"That's okay," Nancy replied. "This is our favorite place. I'll get a drink and check back in a while."

She stood in line at the bar, eventually ordering a Whiskey Sour. With a drink in hand, she made her way to the counter, looking out over the bay. Before she could find a high-top chair, her cellphone rang. She glanced at the screen, seeing that it was Beverly, the friend whose parents owned the house in which she was visiting.

"Hi, Bev, what's up?"

"Bad news. My parents just drove up and asked us to accompany them to a seafood restaurant in Ocean City. I'm afraid that will be the end of good times for tonight. Do you want us to pick you up?"

Nancy looked at the full moon over the bay and the delicious seafood being served on the counter.

"Thanks, but I think I'll stick it out here tonight. You guys enjoy the seafood."

Nancy acquired a high-back chair and asked two young men if they might move over so she could get a full view of the moon over the bay.

Before she knew what was happening, one of the fellows took off, and the other cleared a spot for her.

"Thanks. This is one of the best views down the shore."

"Not a problem, glad to oblige."

They sat on high back stools opposite a shelf on which drinks and food were served. The young man looked into Nancy's large brown eyes.

"Do you live at the shore?"

"I wish," she replied. "I am finishing-up my degree at Drexel. I have an apartment in Philly during the school year and live with my folks in Yardley during the summer. I'm staying with friends in Margate but just for the week. I left the house early to hold a table for the group, but one of the girl's parents dropped-in, and it looks like I am stranded here for the night."

"Well, let's see if I can help you make the best of it.

"I'm Josh, by the way. I'm a student at Stockton during the year. In the summer, I work for a company that inspects rides at area amusement parks."

"I'm Nancy," she replied.

Josh treated them to Vodka Martinis, and the two talked easily through two more drinks and a shared order of Capellini Positano, lump crab meat with pasta and marinara sauce.

She explained that she was a journalism major who wanted to work for newspapers or on television as a reporter. Josh asked her if keeping up with all the dishonesty in politics was not challenging.

She reached out, held his hand, and looked into his eyes.

"If it were not for objective reporters, no one would know what is real and what is fiction. That's the main attraction for me."

It was just after 1:00 am when their conversation slowed, and they began to tire over two cappuccinos topped with whipped cream and shaved chocolate.

"Can I offer you a ride?" Josh asked, as he placed his gold American Express card on top of the check.

"That would be great," she replied. "I walked over from my friend's house in Margate, but given the hour and the number of drinks we consumed, riding back sounds good."

The waiter came to the table, processed the check and credit card, and thanked Josh for a generous tip.

"I'm in the parking lot one block over," Josh said.

They looked at the fading moon over the bay, turned, and walked down the steps to the sidewalk. Josh took her hand as they crossed the street and made their way to the lot.

"I'm the 1968 red Camaro. It was my dad's car when he met my mom. He put a ton of money into it to meet today's requirements. He just didn't have the heart to let it go."

"Sounds like a great guy," Nancy replied.

"He was exceptional. Unfortunately, he died from a stroke when I was in high school, and my mom passed away from cancer the next year."

Nancy put her arms around Josh, holding him tight.

"I'm so sorry," she whispered, kissing him softly on the lips.

Josh followed her directions, driving to a large house a few blocks over, next to the beach.

"The house looks dark," she said.

"Why don't you come in, and we can spend a little more time together?"

He left the car, walked around, and opened her door. When she got out, she put her arms around his neck and kissed him passionately.

"That's for the super time at Lamberti's."

As they strolled down a stone walkway towards the house, a white Chevy SUV pulled into the driveway.

"That would be my girlfriends and the parents," Nancy said. "Unfortunately, we'll never get rid of them."

"If you're free tomorrow, I have the day off. Why don't we meet on the beach around 10:00 am? I'm in a small rental on Thirty-Third Street in Ocean City,"

Josh said.

"Sounds like a plan," she responded.

A large man with dark skin stood across the street studying the parting couple. He took several cell phone pictures of them before driving away in a silver Mercedes.

CHAPTER 3

TUESDAY, JULY 23, 2019
OCEAN CITY, NEW JERSEY

Driving from Margate to Ocean City, Nancy had a good feeling about Josh. She was amazed at how quickly the time went by when they were together. They seemed to hit it off with no real effort.

She drove down Thirty-Third street and parked just a few cars from the beach. With a towel in hand, she entered the sand and looked for Josh. She found him sleeping under an umbrella just a few yards from the water.

She got down on her knees and kissed the back of his neck. He opened his eyes to see Nancy dressed in a dark red pullover.

"Sorry to wake you but the ocean looks too inviting to miss out. I thought you might want to go for a swim."

Josh sat up, gazing into her eyes.

"So glad you could make it. A swim sounds good. The tide is from the south, which means the water temperature should be refreshingly cool."

He stood as Nancy removed her cover-up. She wore a light blue bikini, leaving nothing to the imagination. She could have been a model, firm, and well proportioned.

She glanced at Josh, noting his muscular build, full head of brown hair, and bright blue eyes.

With the lifeguards not on duty until 10:30 am, the crowd was sparse while the ocean offered its full array of challenges.

"Are you up for some body surfing?" he asked. "If we can get out beyond the breakers, there could be some excellent rides."

They waded up to their waists and then swam out towards the waves coming in. There were a couple of minutes between the breakers, allowing them to work their way out. Finally, they could see clear sailing, and they lay on their backs, waiting for a suitable candidate to come in.

"You see that sand bar way out?" Josh asked. "That's the source of the good ones. Just keep your eyes on it, and you'll have time to get ready."

It didn't take long for a wave to escape the sand bar and build-up.

"Here comes one," Josh yelled. "Wait until you

feel it pulling you out to sea and then kick like crazy."

Exactly as promised, the wave began to pull them out, only to see the couple lay flat on their stomachs and begin kicking, arms stretched to the shore. The crest lifted them high above the calm waters and thrust them towards the sand. Although the ride lasted no more than ten seconds, the exhilaration provided made it feel like an hour.

Floating on to the sand, they stood and looked out to sea, not seeing another wave of the same size and intensity.

"That's the best ride I've ever had," Nancy said.

"I think the crest was seven or eight feet above the bottom," Josh added.

"Where is your apartment?" Nancy asked. "I wouldn't mind a break in the action, maybe grabbing lunch after a while."

******

At 1:00 pm., they were sitting in a booth at Kessels Corner, an old-fashioned luncheonette just a couple of blocks from Josh's apartment.

"Walking into Kessels is like walking into the 1950s. Young kids have lunch here without their parents. Burgers and fries are the best anywhere," Josh said.

The two sat quietly, waiting for a waitress to take their order. Both were exhausted and exhilarated from the sex they enjoyed at the apartment. With Nancy on top, she claimed that, once again, she was riding the wave that transported her to unprecedented joy.

Josh remembered looking into her eyes, feeling her pleasure before he became lost in the delectation.

Sitting next to each other in the booth, soon, a waitress approached. Before long, they were enjoying cheeseburgers and shared an order of fries. Nancy drank a chocolate shake and Josh an orange-crème soda.

"This is my third and last summer working at the Jersey Shore," Josh said. "The money I make at Shore Ride Consultants, assisting maintenance supervisors at boardwalk amusement parks, will pay for tuition during my senior year at nearby Stockton University. The skills and techniques I'm learning for my degree in architecture apply to work observing ride stresses, testing metal components, and making suggestions to replace parts or make vital adjustments."

"So, tell me about your journalism studies," Josh said. "Do you want to write material for others or deliver it in newspaper articles or on TV yourself?"

Nancy sucked the last bit of shake up the straw, wiping her mouth with a napkin.

"I'm working on my senior year project. Last year, I did a semester abroad in Jordan. I've always been fascinated by the Middle East, its ancient history and the little they've learned in terms of establishing democracies and broad-based economic prosperity.

"Anyway, I became interested in the Dead Sea Scrolls. Bedouin shepherds discovered most of them in a series of eleven caves in 1947. They're considered the most incredible archeological find ever.

"Most archeologists are interested in the hundreds of leather scrolls found and their contribution to our understanding of Christianity and Judaism. My interest and my paper will focus on a copper scroll and its directions to the treasure. It was found as part of a 1952 expedition by Jordan's Department of Antiquities.

"The scroll is a list of sixty-four locations where, supposedly, huge amounts of silver, gold, and rare antiquities were hidden. We are talking about tons of valuable ore and rare religious ornaments worth billions of dollars in today's money.

"The scroll was found in the back of Cave No. 3, behind a hidden wall, resting on a manmade shelf. Most believe the copper scroll was placed in the cave independently of the Dead Sea scrolls."

Josh interrupted her presentation.

"So, what is the object of your paper? Given the thousands of years since its discovery and the stated value of the treasure, I would think many archeologists have investigated the scroll with the aim of finding the treasure. What would an American reporter add?"

"Well, that's exactly the point," Nancy said. "The challenge is to accumulate enough knowledge to understand the scroll and its implications and then to find and express a new angle...something that would form the basis of an interesting newspaper feature story or a report on the nightly news or even an hour-long TV special."

"Do we know who wrote the scroll?" Josh asked.

"There are many theories. The one that makes the most sense to me speculates that when the Jews feared the destruction of the Second Temple by the Romans in 70 A.D., they hid their valuables and kept track of them through the scroll. In that case, it would have been written by the Temple's treasurer."

"So," Josh asked, "has anyone been able to find the sixty-four locations and recover part of the treasure?"

Nancy looked towards the counter and noticed a long line of patrons waiting for a booth.

"Let's open up our booth to the folks in line and go back to your apartment. Then, we can relax on the beach and continue our conversation.

"And by the way, this is my treat."

CHAPTER 4
TUESDAY, JULY 23, 2019
OCEAN CITY, NEW JERSEY

The couple strolled along the sidewalk, enjoying summer scenes of kids anticipating the fun of the beach and ocean just a few blocks away. Often, they were accompanied by moms and dads with carts overfull of umbrellas, beach toys, rafts, and kites.

"Not to be too critical, but your apartment seems a little out of place among the new, shiny townhouses on Thirty-Third Street," Nancy said.

"I know," Josh responded. "The owner lives upstairs in the summer and rents out the first floor. Although it is an old wooden building, it has all the necessities, and there is plenty of room for a single. And, best of all, the rate is low enough for a struggling graduate student to afford."

They turned the corner across the street from the rental, spotting a large, dark-skinned man leaving the house.

It took Josh a few seconds to react, eventually yelling at the intruder.

"Hey, buddy, what do you think you're doing?"

The man looked to be in his forties, wearing a black shirt and slacks. He turned to Josh and Nancy with a look of rage. Then, he ran to the corner and got in a silver Mercedes that sped away.

Josh and Nancy crossed the street, and Josh opened the front door. They walked in to find that the house had been ransacked. Although there appeared to be nothing missing, Josh's school and work papers had been examined, closets opened, the bed stripped, and kitchen cabinets searched.

"How did he get in?" Nancy asked.

Josh examined the front door lock.

"No sign of tampering here. Let me check the door that leads to the small courtyard along the side."

"Bingo! It looks like he jumped the picket fence to the courtyard and forced the lock on the side door.

"The question in my mind is, what the hell was he looking for. He ignored a twenty-dollar bill on my nightstand that I use for coffee and bakery on workday mornings. So, money wasn't the object."

Nancy sat down at the kitchen table.

"I think I may have been the target. My family's home in Yardley was broken into a week or two after

I moved in this summer. The same result...nothing taken."

"Did your folks call the police?"

"They did, but their investigation came up empty."

"Do you have any idea what they're after?" Josh asked.

Nancy got a glass of water and sat back down. She took a healthy drink and began.

"I know it may sound far-fetched, but this may be associated with my work on the copper scroll. Understand that the descriptions in the scroll concerning where the treasure rests are almost useless.

"For example, one of the sixty-four instructions tells searchers to look in the salt pit that is under the steps where there are forty-one talents of silver. Another instruction points to the cave of the old washer's chamber on the third terrace, where there are sixty-five ingots of gold.

"The simple truth is there is no way to track down these clues after thousands of years. For the most part, you are talking about sites that have been reduced to stone. It is impossible to tell whether the treasure's locations are in Jerusalem, Jericho, or Qumran, in the West Bank, or near the Dead Sea. If you don't know the general geography, how do you follow the specific instructions?"

"So, has anyone found any part of the treasure?" Josh asked.

"In a word, *no*. At least, no one has admitted to finding any part of the treasure. In 1962, an archeologist named John Allegro took advantage of an unpublished account of the scroll and searched the West Bank for locations that appeared to coincide with the scroll's content. He returned empty-handed."

"Okay, so what might our friend be looking for in my apartment? Do you have new clues that point the way to the treasure?"

Nancy took another drink and looked Josh in the eye.

"You must remember that I'm not looking for the treasure. I'm looking for a story that will catch the interest of newspaper editors and TV producers. I concluded months ago that the sixty-four locations were useless. In fact, it occurred to me that the scroll may have been written to lead treasure hunters away from the antiquities and bullion that could well rest in a single, remote location.

"Anyway, just before I began my summer break, I drove to Princeton to meet with Professor Samuel Wadsworth. He is the Director of Research for the Princeton Theological Seminary. He had just returned from a trip to Jordan to meet with an antiquities dealer, a man he saved from three thugs when he was a student. He is working on a new translation of the scroll, one that he claims will put the information in a unique context."

"Did he provide you with any documentation, something that would get the attention of treasure hunters?"

"He did not. All I walked away with were my taped notes."

Nancy reached into her purse and produced an Olympus digital voice recorder, about half the size of an average cell phone.

"I guess this could have been the target. But I've been through the interview many times and haven't been able to find any new or vital information."

"Let's put my apartment back together. Then, we can sit and listen to the interview. Maybe someone not previously involved in the subject matter can come up with a clue," Josh said.

CHAPTER 5
TUESDAY, JULY 23, 2019
OCEAN CITY, NEW JERSEY

An hour later, the couple was back on the beach. They reasoned that if someone wanted to eavesdrop on their conversation, given the background noise near the ocean, they would be assured of privacy. They sat close under the umbrella on a wide beach blanket.

"Okay, here we go," Nancy said as she pushed the playback button.

Josh looked into her eyes as they listened intently. He couldn't help replaying their love making as the tape progressed through her interview. Then, he thought he noticed something.

He reached out and held her wrist.

"Hold on a second. Can you replay the last few sentences?"

Nancy backed up the tape and hit play.

"Professor, are you preparing a new description

of the scroll? If so, can you tell me how it will differ from earlier versions?"

There was an unusually long pause as the Professor thought through his response.

"I have access to new, sharper image photographs of the scroll taken by associates in Great Britain. They have provided the pictures on the condition that my new edition covers all the sixty-four locations in a unified manner."

"So, we are talking about accounts of the sixty-four locations and how they might relate to one another?" Nancy asked.

"As I think you know, the sixty-fourth location includes a guide to help interpret the others. Unfortunately, it has never been found," the professor added.

Josh interrupted the playback of the tape.

"Go back again," he suggested. "Notice how his voice appears to change when he talks about the sixty-fourth location and about finding the guide.

"When I was an undergraduate, I took an elective course in criminology as a summer fill-in. There is something called verbal leakage that occurs during deceptive responses. The voice frequency changes involuntarily due to the stress of a dishonest or deceptive answer. If you listen to it, the audio range of vocal transmissions is detectable by the human ear.

"I wouldn't bet my life on it, but it sounds to me like your friend in Princeton may have the guide promised by the sixty-fourth document.

"There is a computer program at Stockton's Criminology Department that will assess voice frequency and supply indications of disingenuous responses or speech. If you agree, I'll call my professor and see if we can get access for an hour or two."

******

Two days later, Josh and Nancy drove to the Stockton campus, about forty minutes from Ocean City. It was early morning when the Department agreed to the use of the frequency analytic program. A graduate assistant met them in the lab that housed the program.

Josh and Nancy walked in, spotting a young man with shoulder-length hair.

"Hi, I'm Josh Rosenberg, and this is Nancy Troll. Professor Clint was kind enough to allow our restricted use of the voice frequency program."

The assistant met them with a polite wave.

"This is not the usual routine, but I understand that you completed Criminology 102 last year and that you are a graduate student in Stockton Architecture. So, I guess we're good to go. Can I see what we're to examine?"

Nancy removed the recorder from her purse and handed it to the assistant.

"It's an interview I conducted about upcoming research on the Dead Sea Scrolls. I'm a journalism major at Drexel, and my senior project involves new studies that may become available. We're not sure if the information provided in the interview is straight or not."

"Who did you interview?" asked the assistant.

Nancy and Josh had agreed before the session not to reveal the name of the Director, removing any reference to him on the tape.

"He's a researcher in Princeton, at the University."

"So, you think he may be lying?" asked the staffer.

"No, that's not it," Nancy replied. "We think he may not have clearance to reveal information about future plans. If that's the case, I'll know where to direct my next inquiries."

The tape was played three times, and the transmission was charted in terms of frequency. Each time, the section of the interview dealing with the sixty-fourth location and the guide was flagged as deceptive.

"Does that confirm your suspicions?" asked the Stockton assistant.

"Yes, it does," Nancy responded. "Thanks so much for your help. Now I know how to continue my research."

They recovered the tape recorder and walked out to the hallway of the red brick building. This was Stockton's original campus. With growing student interest in attending the school and little land open for further expansion, the university began work on a second campus, this one near the beach in Atlantic City.

They walked down the stairs and out the main doors. Then, around to the rear of the building where its parking lot was located. Because it was still early morning in the summer, the campus seemed almost empty.

"So, what's your next step?" Josh asked.

"I think I'll make a surprise visit to Professor Wadsworth in Princeton. If I can get in to see him, I think I'll tell him that I've received a report that the guide from the sixty-fourth instruction has been found and ask for his reaction."

"What if he asks who the author of the report is?"

"I'll simply plead confidentiality of my source."

"Exactly what does the copper scroll say in its sixty-fourth instruction, that is, less the guide itself?" Josh asked.

Nancy removed a notebook from her backpack, flipped through several pages, and began reading:

"In a pit adjoining on the north, in a hole

opening northward, and buried at its mouth is a guide, providing an explanation of each treasure entry and their measurements, an inventory of each and every thing."

"That's it. Some are convinced that if you have the guide of the sixty-fourth instruction, you can find the treasure."

"Are you heading back to Yardley?" Josh asked.

Nancy turned to Josh, putting her arms around him.

"I thought I might return to your apartment and the beach on Thirty-Third. Maybe try Kessels for dinner?"

"Super idea."

CHAPTER 6
SUNDAY, JULY 28, 2019
OCEAN CITY, NEW JERSEY

After another intense day and night together, Nancy returned to Yardley and Josh to his summer job. Nancy planned to drive to Princeton on Monday to confront Professor Wadsworth.

Josh had Nancy promise to call him and provide the results of her session as soon as it was concluded. Thus far, except for the two break-ins, there was no sign of violence. However, given his growing feelings for this bright and adventuresome young woman and the potential value of the copper scroll's sixty-fourth text and guide, Josh didn't want to take any chances.

******

On Monday, driving the backroads to Princeton, Nancy went over her script along the quiet streets that navigated through Lawrenceville and then to the rustic campus of the Princeton Theological Seminary on Mercer Street.

She pulled into the tree-lined avenue and parked in the lot alongside the light brick building housing the campus headquarters. The seminary is housed in a long structure with a central portico, white pillars, and a white cupola sporting a border fence and rounded metal dome.

Still sitting behind the wheel, she rehearsed the key question she would be asking.

"Professor, I really appreciate your information, but one of my sources claims that the sixty-fourth instruction and guide have been found. If that's the case, will you be able to use them in your interpretation of the scroll?"

She showed her press credentials to the security guard at the entrance and went ahead to Wadsworth's office, where she claimed she had an appointment.

Carol sat outside his closed door, transcribing material from a recent lecture. Spotting Nancy, she removed her earphones and interrupted her work.

"Nice to see you again," she said. "Did you have issues from your interview that require clarification?"

Relieved by the friendly reception, Nancy pursued her goal.

"It's great to see you again. Yes, you hit the nail on the head. I have a few follow-up issues that need resolution. The professor was so nice I didn't think he'd mind giving me a little time to clear things up."

"The only problem is that he works Monday mornings at home. Let me check-in and see if you can visit with him there."

The secretary called his number. After several rings, there was no response.

"That's strange. He must be tied-up with something. Why don't you come back at 2:00 pm, and I'll write you on to his calendar."

"Thanks so much, Nancy replied. The delay will give me an opportunity to do some shopping in Princeton."

Rather than wait, she thought this might be an even better opportunity to confront the professor in an unconventional setting. Using her cell phone, she found the professor's home address and the route from her current location. He lived just three blocks from the Seminary campus on a thickly wooded cul-de-sac.

Following her cell phone map, she made her way to the professor's street and home address. She parked in front of a stone house of Georgian design on an avenue of well-spaced million-dollar houses.

Nancy scooped up her tablet from the passenger seat and opened her car door, beginning to exit.

With no warning, a thunderous blast and blazing fireball took over the environment. Feeling her face burning, she fell back into her car, closing the door, praying that the car wouldn't explode.

She felt herself lose conscientiousness, her head falling forwards towards the floor of the vehicle. Several minutes later, she awoke, still feeling the extreme heat of the explosion. She raised herself up to look at the house she could have been in when it was destroyed.

Dizzy from the concussion, she searched through her purse for her cell phone. Before she could dial 911, she dropped the device onto the floor. Then, she heard the sirens.

Within the next sixty seconds, two police cars and four fire engines arrived. The firemen connected their hoses to a plug located in front of the Wadsworth house and directed broad streams of water into the blaze.

"Ma'am, are you alright?"

One of the police officers had opened her car door.

Nancy tried to answer, but no words escaped her mouth.

"Ma'am, I believe you are in shock. An ambulance will be here any second. You need to be checked-out at the hospital. Just stay quiet. I'll stay with you until you can be on your own or call a relative to pick you up."

The next few hours were a blur. Nancy was diagnosed with a mild concussion. She had some facial burns from the blast but overall was protected by the car's windshield.

The police officer, Officer Jacobs, called the house in Yardley but got no answer. Eventually, Nancy remembered that her folks had left on a five-day holiday to the Greenbrier resort in West Virginia.

Instead of calling her parents on their cellphones and interrupting their vacation, Nancy said she would prefer to call her boyfriend down the shore. He would drive her home.

With Officer Jacobs sitting on a chair in her hospital room, Nancy speed-dialed Josh.

He recognized her number and picked up right away.

"How are you? How did your interview go?"

"I'm afraid there was a problem. I had just pulled up in front of Professor Wadsworth's house when a terrible explosion and fire happened. I'm in Princeton Hospital with a concussion. My folks are away on vacation, and I need someone to pick me up and drive me home. I'm wondering if you might skip work and do me the favor."

"Is Wadsworth dead?" Josh asked.

"My God, I don't know. If he was in the house, there's no way he could have survived."

She turned to Jacobs.

"Officer, do you know if Professor Wadsworth

was home, and if he was, did he survive the explosion?"

"I'm afraid there's bad news on both accounts. The professor was home and no, he didn't survive."

Nancy's mind was blitzed by too many questions. Was the gas explosion an accident or a way to cut off Wadsworth's report on the sixty-fourth location and its guide? The explosion was the kind of overkill typical of Middle East violence.

Given her interview with the victim and her presence at the house, will she be next? Are there clues to Wadsworth's breakthrough in his office or what's left of his house?

Nancy shifted her attention back to her telephone conversation.

"No, the Professor didn't make it," she said, tearing up.

"Stay put in the hospital, and I'll be there in a couple of hours," Josh said. "Once I get you home, we'll figure out what to do next."

After Nancy ended her call with Josh, Officer Jacobs said goodbye, wishing her a speedy recovery. Then, a doctor and nurse came in to make sure her symptoms had stabilized. While the doctor preferred that she stay the night, he understood her preference to go home. However, she would have to sign a release form, removing the hospital from any liability.

Before she could get comfortable again, two

detectives from the State police entered the room. Both were middle-aged and appeared to be veterans of the force.

"Ma'am, I am Detective Moore, and this is Detective Statelmyer. We're both with the Investigations Unit of the State Police. If you are well enough, we have several questions we need to ask you."

"I'm happy to help," Nancy said. "I can't believe the Professor is dead. I just met with him a month ago. He was so nice and cooperative."

"So, what was the purpose of your meeting a month ago, and what were you doing at his house today?" asked Detective Moore.

"I'm a student at Drexel, majoring in Journalism. My senior project involves research on the Dead Sea Scrolls, and the Professor helped me interpret the information I acquired. After I had a chance to absorb his contributions and gain some other information, I had some follow-up questions for him. His secretary said he was working at home today, so I took the liberty of trying to hook-up with him there."

"What's a journalism major doing studying the Dead Sea Scrolls?" asked Detective Statelmyer.

"The idea is to find a topic and do research that might form the basis of a newspaper article or series or TV nightly news report or special. I spent my semester abroad in the Middle East, mostly in Jordan, and was fascinated by stories about the scrolls."

"Did you see or hear anything outside the Professor's house just before the explosion?"

"I had just pulled up in front when I grabbed my tablet and opened the car door. That's when all hell broke loose. No, other than the blast, I heard nothing."

"Is there anything about the Professor's research or your studies that could be a motive for violence?" Detective Moore inquired.

"Do you think the blast was intentional? I assumed it was from an accidental gas leak," Nancy said.

"At this point in our investigation, all possibilities are on the table," Moore replied.

"Is there any reason you can see that would justify violence against Professor Wadsworth?"

Nancy wasn't sure how she should handle his question. If she raised the issue of the sixty-fourth text and guide and how they might lead to an incredible treasure, she might open the door to many other researchers and journalists. That was the last thing she wanted to do.

On the other hand, skirting the issue altogether could lead to charges against her.

"You know, Detective, these scrolls are thousands of years old. They have been the subject of research by some of the best archeologists in the world. It's hard to believe that anything new could be discovered and might lead to some kind of violence."

After thanking her for answering their questions while still in hospital, they wished her well and left. However, they said they might have some other inquiries once more information becomes available.

Nancy knew she was walking a tightrope. The violence she saw in the Professor's house explosion was, unfortunately, typical of Middle East terrorists who had no consideration for life when it got in the way of their objectives. If she kept digging into the scroll and its treasure, she might be setting herself up as another target. On the other hand, the risks she knew she would take could pay off with a newsworthy story and recognition as an up-and-coming reporter.

PART TWO
SEARCHING THE LANDSCAPE

CHAPTER 7
MONDAY, JULY 29, 2019
TRENTON, NEW JERSEY

Detectives Moore and Statelmyer drove back to their office within the State Police Investigations Branch in Trenton, New Jersey's capital city. Moore had black hair combed straight back and black-rimmed glasses that gave him a studious appearance. Statelmyer was tall with an athletic build and sharp blue eyes. Both men had been with Investigations for ten years, and both were first-rate officers.

Driving back to the office, they agreed that the gas explosion and fire fell within the investigations mission to prevent, disrupt, interdict, and investigate violent and organized criminals, terrorism, corruption, and casino-related crime. The fact that Wadsworth had been beheaded before the explosion led them to believe they were dealing with an act of terrorism. Given the nature of the crime and the professor's most recent work, they wondered if the perpetrators might be related to sources in the Middle East.

Sitting at the conference table while eating Jersey Mike's hoagies for supper, they discussed the next steps.

"We need to lay this out for Commander Auburn," Moore said. "He'll want a clear path of suggested steps."

"Agree," Statelmyer responded. "First, we need detailed forensics about the scene of the crime. How many were involved? How was he beheaded? How was the gas explosion generated? And we need to get our hands on any neighborhood video before and after the killing."

"I got a quick look at the *Trenton Times* for this evening. They're assuming this was some kind of gas line accident," Moore said.

"That's fine," Statelmyer responded. "Once they get a hold of the beheading, in Princeton of all places, within a staid religious organization, the pressure will be shades of nine/eleven."

******

It was after eight o'clock on Monday night when Josh arrived at the Princeton Hospital on Route #1. He found his way to Nancy's room, knocked, and entered. He was shocked by her pale and weakened appearance.

Josh walked to her bedside, placed his hands

under her back, and lifted her close.

"I've been so worried. I love you."

"I love you too," Nancy whispered. "Please, get me out of here."

After dressing, signing the required waiver, and getting her things together, a nurse asked that she sit in a wheelchair and be pushed to the parking lot circle entrance. By the time an orderly transported her to the hospital door, Josh had already pulled his car into the circle and entered her parent's address into his cellphone's GPS system.

Josh exited the Camaro and escorted Nancy to the passenger door.

"You need to rest," he said. "Do you want to lie down on the back seat or sit here next to me?"

"Next to you sounds good," she responded.

Within the next ten minutes, Nancy was fast asleep. An hour later, Josh pulled his car into her parents' driveway. An hour after that, she was asleep in her bedroom. Thinking of the break-ins, Josh lay in her bed, wondering if the explosion was an accident or some kind of attack related to the copper scroll.

******

Commander Auburn sat at the head of the conference table. It was 11:30 at night, an unusual time for such a meeting. However, as soon as he learned of the beheading, he called all the right staff together.

Auburn was tall and slender with styled red hair. He was promoted to Commander while in his forties, mainly due to his calm and analytic approach to complex cases. He had a perceptive ability to sort out political elements that could have far-reaching implications in the future.

In addition to Moore and Statelmyer, Eleanor Williams, the Department's Director of Forensics, and Barry Rank, Chief of the Princeton Fire Department, sat around the table.

"I'm sorry for the late hour, but something tells me this case won't wait for routine hours," Auburn said. "Now, I need to know what you know before I call-in the federal authorities.

"Eleanor, let's begin with you. What do the forensics tell us?"

Eleanor was an African American professional with close to twenty years of experience. Her sharp perception was matched with advanced skills in the laboratory she managed. She addressed Auburn while also looking at the others around the table.

"The gas explosion scrambled and, in some instances, destroyed much of the evidence. On the other hand, fumes blew up in the basement, quite far from the site of the murder. Although the body and nearby furnishings were charred, there was enough left to put the scene together.

"First, the Professor was tied to a chair in his first-floor office and tortured before he was beheaded, and the gas ignited. Although he was found lying on his side, one of the straps on his right ankle remained in place around what was left of the leg of a chair.

"Second, based on blood loss, the beheading appears to have happened while the victim was still alive. Some kind of heavy sword would have been used, swung by an extremely strong individual.

"Based upon what I can remember from forensic history, beheadings, and separated heads were used as warnings to strike fear into opposition forces back in biblical times. This is the first beheading I've seen since I began practicing twenty years ago. Of course, we saw ISIS use this tactic not too many years ago in the Middle East.

"Third, given the coordinated explosion and murder, I would guess at least three individuals were actively involved."

Auburn turned to Barry Rank of the Princeton Fire Department.

"As Eleanor noted, the explosion happened in the basement. We found evidence of a timer that ignited the gas that flowed in from an intentionally created gap in the pipe that carried fuel into the house. This was a sloppy job."

"In what respects was it sloppy?" Auburn

asked.

"Well, when we investigate the scene of such an explosion, if it's intentional, efforts are made to disguise the cause so the insurance company will pay up. In this case, there were no such signs."

"So, based on what I'm hearing so far," Auburn concluded, "the house invasion was to extract information from the Professor. Then, when that failed, the murder and explosion appear to have been executed as a warning to another party or group. Does that correspond with your assessments?"

All nodded in agreement.

Auburn turned to Moore and Statelmyer.

"Okay, guys, now for the hard part. What kind of motive are we looking at? What would lead to such violence within the confines of Princeton's peaceful and educated community?"

Detective Moore took the lead.

"The short answer is, we don't know. We're going to have to get into his work and find out if the Professor's research and travels provide a clue. This means spending some time at the Seminary and questioning his associates."

Statelmyer chimed in.

"I want to go back and interview the young woman who was at the site of the explosion in her car. It was obvious that she was holding back."

"Okay, folks, thanks for your information. I have enough to inform our FBI and CIA liaisons and see if they want to come on board. I'll schedule another meeting a day or two from now, and we can review what new information has been developed.

"If you are questioned by the news media, "No comment" is the only proper response. After I have a chance to discuss things with the Feds, we'll hold a press conference.

"Thank you, and good night."

CHAPTER 8

TUESDAY, JULY 30, 2019
YARDLEY, PENNSYLVANIA

Josh and Nancy awoke at 8:00 am, made love, and fell back asleep. They didn't get out of bed until 11:00 am. Nancy showered, got dressed, and made coffee as Josh showered, called his boss to explain why he wouldn't be back at work for a day or so, and joined Nancy in the kitchen.

Sitting at the breakfast nook, Nancy tried to think through her situation.

"Besides returning to the scene of the crime to get my car, I'm not sure how to proceed. Do I continue pressing ahead with my story, focusing on the treasure, or do I expand things to incorporate the explosion and the Professor's death? Or do I level with the police and abandon the project because of the danger posed by whoever broke into our houses and may have been responsible for the gas explosion and fire?"

Josh poured a second cup of coffee while understanding that his advice could have important consequences.

"I don't know about the supposed treasure. It may or may not exist. My gut tells me that covering those still hooked on its promise could provide you with an interesting story for your project. On the other hand, if that means being a target for violence, no story or school project is worth that.

"Can you run all this by your mentor at Drexel, get his advice?"

"That's a great idea," Nancy replied. "The problem is my professor is in Jordan working on his own research. He asked to be left alone until he returns in August."

"Speaking strictly as a lay person and putting aside the fact that I am in love with you, you are in a unique position to pursue what could be a big story. Regarding the treasure, you have evidence that suggests the existence of new information to pinpoint its location. Then, mix in the two break-ins, the gas explosion, and Wadsworth's death. They add a whole new dimension to the feature. If you were a hardened reporter, I think it would be full speed ahead."

"So, you're saying the hell with the danger, just pursue the story?"

"The thing is, that gas explosion and the death

of Professor Wadsworth have brought the police into the equation. It would be foolish for those looking to cash-in on the treasure to murder a student reporter."

"So, you think I should keep working."

Josh looked into Nancy's eyes, feeling his dependence on her caring and the physical pleasure they shared.

"I guess, if it were me, I'd proceed slowly and as quietly as possible. Look into Wadsworth's plans and try to figure out where he was heading. Compile as much information as you can about the explosion and fire. Hell, you have the unique distinction of being there as it happened. When you have a fair idea of what it's all about, write it up as a page one newspaper article or series of articles that might form the basis of an hour-long TV special, with video from Princeton and the Middle East. Then, run it by your mentor and go from there."

The couple was quiet as Josh drove them back to Princeton to retrieve Nancy's car. He was beginning to have second thoughts, not wanting to suffer regret if his advice led to physical harm. Nancy, thinking about the potential of the story, was leaning the opposite way. She was having dreams of a network job following her breaking news.

Nancy directed Josh to Wadsworth's block, where she left her car. They looked at the massive destruction that left the house in shambles. Then, they realized that her vehicle was gone.

"Do you think the police impounded the car?" Nancy asked.

"It wouldn't surprise me," Josh responded. "What were the names of the detectives you met at the hospital? They should know if the car was taken in."

As Josh and Nancy sat in the Camaro using their cell phones to locate a number for Detective Moore, a silent drone flew overhead. It photographed their vehicle and recorded the couple's conversations. When they left the scene to retrieve Nancy's car, the drone continued to circle the crime scene, reaching out for clues.

A brief discussion with Detective Moore's assistant led them to an impoundment lot in Trenton. The car had been towed as evidence in a crime scene. However, Moore had left word that the car could be released to the owner with no charge.

With Nancy sitting behind the wheel, ready to drive home, Josh stood next to her open window.

"So, what have you decided?"

"I'm going to drive home and put together a list of parties to interview. Then, I'm going to go after the story. What started as a remote and technical endeavor could be my ticket to the big time, thanks in part to your perspective."

Josh reached inside the car, kissing her on the lips.

"Just be careful. If you feel you are in danger, step away and call one of your detective friends. If you want, I can come back for the weekend."

"Let's see how things go. I may want to visit you for the weekend. My parents will be home, and your place, with the beach and Kessels so close, is hard to resist."

They kissed again, and each went their own way.

CHAPTER 9

Nancy and Carol Stark, Wadsworth's secretary, sat together in the lounge that served Seminary staff. Carol had worked for the Professor for three years. Her husband was a salesman for a lab testing firm just outside Princeton. Their two children were in one of Princeton's finer elementary schools. She respected Wadsworth and found him easy to work for. In fact, until the explosion, she saw herself working with the professor for many more years.

As she described her supervisor and friend, tears rolled down her cheeks.

"He was the sweetest man, so considerate of me and the demands kids make these days. He never denied me a day or afternoon off to attend school events. With no wife of his own, I first thought he might be tough to work for. But it was just the opposite."

Nancy searched for information that could be relevant to her project.

"Do you know if the Professor had any repair work on his house recently? Sometimes, gas explosions follow careless workers."

"I don't think so," Carol replied.

"Would you say that his work has been pretty routine lately?" she asked.

Carol paused, beginning to feel uncomfortable.

"What are you getting at? He was conducting his research and writing up the findings as always. I received a call from a detective with the New Jersey State Police this morning. He said they wanted to talk to me about the Professor. I don't understand what's going on."

Nancy wasn't sure how much she should reveal but felt she owed Carol an explanation.

"The truth is that although the Professor's research dealt with antiquities from thousands of years ago, sometimes, new findings can have political or even monetary consequences. When I met with him, we discussed scrolls that have supplied immense information about how the early Jews and Christians lived.

"Was he excited about his work the last few days?"

Carol began to withdraw, not certain where this

was heading.

"You're probably better off asking those kinds of questions of research staff who assisted him. Most of his work went through the President of the Seminary, Doctor Parnes. He would have the best sense of the Professor's progress.

"I'm sorry to cut this off, but I need to go home and change for the memorial service being conducted this afternoon."

"Of course," Nancy replied, feeling somewhat guilty.

"You have my sincere sympathies. Please let me know if there's anything I can do to help."

Nancy stood, hugged Carol, turned, and walked away, heading to the exit and her car. Carol, unsure of her future course, sat for several minutes wondering how she should conduct herself. The Friday before the explosion, the Professor handed a thick manilla envelope to her marked *Eyes Only*. She remembered his exact words.

"I just received this package from the antiquities dealer I know in Amman. I don't want to burden any of the staff or Director Parnes with these findings. I'd appreciate it if you would take this home and put it in a safe place. I'll take it off your hands on Monday afternoon."

Nancy drove into town, parked in a metered lot,

and purchased a sandwich from Panera's on Nassau Street. Then, she walked across the street and on to the stately Princeton campus, found a strategically located bench, and tried to relax.

Although Carol was friendly and cooperative, when pressed, she appeared to hold back. Knowing when a source had more to give was an important skill for veteran reporters.

She decided to attend the memorial service scheduled to take place in the huge, ornate campus cathedral. Her bench was just outside the entrance, and she would get a good look at all those attending, beginning in a half hour.

A trickle of early attendees became a long line of distinguished looking academics, clergy, and saddened students. Carol and her husband arrived just before the doors closed and the service began. Nancy had press credentials given to her by her university Department but wasn't asked to produce them.

Nancy sat in the last row of seats with many of Wadsworth's students. She looked around at the beautiful sculptures, stained glass windows, and exquisite paintings. Combining the University surroundings with the Seminary's religious teachings and antiquities research must have been a dream environment for the Professor. This was an end no one could have predicted.

After three speakers praised the Professor for his brilliance and dedication, the congregation was asked to stand for a closing hymn and prayer.

A cold stare took Nancy's breath away. The dark man who had broken into Josh's beach apartment was there, sitting at the end of an aisle near the front of the church. He appeared to be surveying those in attendance, looking for individuals who might threaten his schemes, whatever they were. She moved closer to a young man in their row, hoping to disappear in the crowd.

As soon as the proceedings ended, she walked directly to her car and drove home. Nancy was anxious to see if the man would attend tomorrow's news conference scheduled by the New Jersey State Police.

CHAPTER 10

The press conference was held in the late afternoon in a modest-sized conference room at the State Police Investigations Headquarters. No more than a dozen members of the press were in attendance, waiting for the session to begin.

Nancy sat at the back of the room in the last of twenty rows of chairs. She hoped the meeting would help fill in some of the blanks that were dominating her academic project, as well as her life. Could the police explain how the Professor lost his life? Did his research lead to his death? Did they know why a student reporter was being followed and why the homes of her parents and friend were searched?

Ironically, the members of the press who needed to be there passed up the session for other duties. This was due to the impression left by the police and fire departments and the Trenton Times. All appeared to conclude that the fire was the result of a random gas leak and an unlucky spark. The death of the Professor was the accidental result of the explosion and fire.

Therefore, those scattered around the room were reporters who followed fires, the religious doings and research of the Seminary, and personal stories about exceptional and influential personalities who died prematurely. Reporters who specialized in murder and terror would have to receive vital information about to be offered on tape, on a secondhand basis, or through later interviews.

It was twenty minutes past the 3:00 pm start scheduled when Commander Auburn, Detectives Moore and Statelmyer, Fire Chief Rank, and Forensics Director Williams entered the room. Auburn approached the microphone, not really needed, given the limited size of the audience.

"Good afternoon.

"My purpose today is to provide you with what we know about the tragic death of Professor Samuel Wadsworth. Then, we will be available to respond to your questions.

"I want to emphasize that under normal circumstances, we might have withheld much of the information I am about to release. However, we want to dispel any speculation that there are dangerous problems with the area's gas lines. Also, the nature of the crime indicates that this was not a random occurrence but was based upon specific relations between the Professor and those involved. There appears to be no threat of violence to the public."

Puzzled looks descended on the reporters present.

Auburn took a sip of water.

"At 12:04 pm on Monday, July 29, a gas explosion and fire destroyed the home of Professor Samuel Wadsworth. Prior to that incident, the Professor was murdered, bound to a chair in his home, and beheaded.

"At this stage in our investigation, we are not aware of any motive for this heinous crime or who might have been the perpetrators.

"We have fully informed staff of the State's terrorism unit, as well as proper sources at the FBI and U.S. Central Intelligence Agency. Each will be provided with daily updates and has expressed an interest in playing a role in our investigation.

"Now, I'd be willing to respond to your questions."

Shock blinded each reporter in the room. Auburn's revelations were so far from what was expected that not a single reporter posed a question. Close to thirty seconds later, Auburn collected his notes and readied to leave the room.

"If there are no questions…"

Before he could finish his sentence, Bob Brice, the Trenton Times religious editor, spoke up.

"Before you leave the room, give us a chance to absorb the shock of this unexpected news.

"Are you saying that the fire was intentionally set?"

Chief Rank moved to the microphone.

"Based upon the evidence, the gas explosion was the result of tampering with the gas line followed by a spark that emanated from a timer device."

Brice continued his questioning.

"So, was the Professor alive when the explosion hit?"

Forensics Director Williams responded.

"The Professor was deceased by the time the explosion and fire consumed his home."

"You said the Professor was beheaded?" Brice continued.

"Yes, he was tied to a chair and beheaded," Williams responded.

Having known and liked the Professor for some time, Brice couldn't force himself to continue his questioning, his mind fighting the images that must have been a horror for his friend.

With those at the session realizing that they were in on what was likely a national story of real significance, the tenor of the room changed.

"My name is Harriet Downey. I'm a reporter with the Trentonian."

Tall and slender with her hair in a bun, she glanced at her notes, taken as the proceedings unfolded.

"Can you tell us how many were involved in the fire and murder?"

Detective Moore moved to the lectern.

"Of course, we are not certain of the number of perpetrators. However, we believe two or three would have been required to set the gas leak, fire, and murder of the Professor."

Downey continued.

"Is there any hint as to a motive? Why would a Seminary Professor be killed in this ghastly manner?"

"The short answer is that we don't know," Moore responded. "We believe the Professor was being interrogated before his murder. However, the subject of the questioning remains a mystery."

Nancy stood, swallowed hard, and added to the questioning.

"Given the way in which the Professor was killed and his research that I believe is based upon Middle East antiquities, will you be investigating the possibility that this crime was carried out by foreign, Middle East elements?"

Auburn moved back to the microphone.

"We will be looking at every possibility, including Middle East sources.

"If you have additional questions, please refer them to Pat Kline of our Information Office. She will be glad to forward your inquiries to the right staff and get you a response.

"Unfortunately, we have another commitment and must end this session. However, we will schedule another conference as developments warrant.

"Thank you for your participation.

"Oh, one more thing; would Nancy Troll remain for a few minutes? I believe Detectives Moore and Statelmyer have a few more questions for you."

As the session ended, most in attendance turned to look for the young lady who was unknown to them.

Nancy tried to appear calm. Inside, however, where she stored the story of treasure and the sixty-fourth instruction and guide of the copper scroll, she couldn't suppress her excitement. The truth was that she knew more about the situation than anyone not directly involved.

The challenge was to keep building her story while staying safe. As far as the police were concerned, she would share what she could without betraying the exclusive knowledge she had developed.

As she assembled her notes, Detective Moore approached.

"Hi, Nancy; please follow me. We need your help."

Moore led her into a small office across the hall from the conference room. Statelmyer was already sitting behind one of three desks.

"Have a seat," he said, pointing to one of the desks.

Nancy noted an enhanced level of seriousness behind the detective's demeanor. She sat at the desk across from Statelmyer and placed her notes down.

"Look," Statelmyer began, "you need to realize that this isn't a game. A respected citizen of Princeton has been murdered in an unspeakable manner, and we need to know why. Our concern is that he may be the first of many. So, you have a responsibility to tell us what's going on."

Nancy could feel a thin layer of sweat form on her upper lip.

"Detective, of course I'm willing to help in any way possible. But realize that I only met with the Professor one time. I had several questions about the Dead Sea Scrolls, on which he is an expert. I don't see how my interview figures into his murder."

Detective Moore took over.

"Specifically, what questions did you pose to the Professor, and what were his answers? Do you have a transcript that we can see?"

Nancy could feel the walls closing in.

Ignoring the tape of their interview in her backpack and thinking first of the exclusive information she would release in her articles, she lied.

"No, I don't have a transcript, just notes that I've combined into a draft summary."

"Okay, with what did your notes deal? Give us a few examples."

"Well, we talked about one of the Dead Sea Scrolls, called the copper scroll. The Professor was researching its origin and meanings. It was supposed to provide the location of treasure, 4,600 religious items made of precious metals, as well as gold and silver bars. However, no one has ever been able to follow the copper scroll to the valuables promised."

The two detectives brightened.

"Now we're getting somewhere," Moore reacted.

"Did he have new information about the treasure?"

"No, he denied any breakthroughs."

"Who might we question to get more details on this research?" Moore asked.

"Apparently, he was reporting directly to Doctor Parnes, Director of the Seminary. He might be your next stop."

Detective Moore summed up.

"Okay, thanks, Nancy. This might be a useful lead. We'll get back to you if we have some follow-up questions."

Sitting in her car, Nancy tried to summarize what had transpired. On the one hand, to a certain extent, she did provide additional information to the detectives, revealing the professor's interest in the copper scroll and its treasure. On the other hand, she withheld the recorded information, wasn't specific about the sixty-fourth instruction and guide, and didn't supply the description of the man who broke into Josh's apartment and was present at the memorial service.

She would drive home and chart out her next steps. Maybe it was time to outline the series of articles that would form the basis of her senior project and move her into the ranks of respected reporters.

CHAPTER 11
SATURDAY, AUGUST 3, 2019
PRINCETON, NEW JERSEY

It was early morning when Carol Stark decided to go into the office and tie up loose ends. She would finish typing the Professor's notes, straighten his office, and then contact Director Parnes to volunteer her services until a replacement was found for her deceased supervisor.

The last thing she wanted to do was get the details of Professor Wadsworth's death. In fact, she was trying to suppress the pictures in her mind of his last-ditch effort to fight the flames that no doubt surrounded him, causing unimaginable pain and death. There was no justice, she thought to herself, a kind, brilliant man dying prematurely in that manner.

Carol finished typing the lecture notes Professor Wadsworth would never deliver and moved into his office. With hundreds of volumes in the bookcases that lined the walls, she could almost feel the loss of expertise his death created. She was no expert in Middle East antiquities but being around the Professor, transcribing his thoughts, left her with more than a minimum of knowledge on certain subjects, especially the Dead Sea Scrolls.

She removed the books from his desk and placed them in their spots in the bookcases around the room. Then, she straightened his desk, discarding notes with incomplete sentences. When Director Parnes visited the office, he would find a neat, well-ordered place of work.

As she was about to take a break, her phone buzzed.

"Hello, this is Carol."

"Carol, this is Marge in Director Parnes' office. If you have a few minutes, he would like to see you."

"Sure, I'll be right up."

Carol figured that the Director may have found an alternative spot for her, at least until Professor Wadsworth's successor was designated. She looked forward to another challenge.

Marge escorted her into Parnes' office, replete with decorative plants and awards that recognized the Seminary for its superior knowledge, research, and religious leadership.

The Director was in his seventies with grey

hair and a grey, closely cut beard. His blue eyes cast a sadness Carol hadn't seen before. He asked her to sit at his conference table. He took a chair opposite hers so he could look directly into her eyes.

"Carol, I'm sorry to be the one to tell you but I wanted you to hear it from me rather than the newspapers, TV, or other staff. According to the police, Professor Wadsworth was…"

He paused and sipped water from a glass in front of him. Then, he poured another glass of water from a white pitcher and placed it in front of Carol. He began again.

"According to the police, Professor Wadsworth was murdered, tied to a chair in his house, tortured, and beheaded. Then, the gas explosion and fire were set to destroy much of the evidence."

Devastated by this new information, Carol drank from the newly poured glass of water and wept uncontrollably. The Director rose from his chair and approached Carol as she stood. The two hugged, comforting one another.

Through her tears, she expressed both sadness and frustration.

"I don't understand. He was an academic, a shining light on antiquities such as the Dead Sea Scrolls. How could such research provide a reason for murder?"

The two separated and sat back down.

The Director took charge of the situation.

"Carol, I want you to take the next week off, get more involved with your wonderful family, and try to forget Dr. Wadsworth's tragedy. I'll try to find a new spot for you when you return, a week from Monday. In the meantime, if you need anything at all, don't hesitate to call me."

The two stood, hugged again, and Carol left for home.

Along the way, she remembered the *Eyes-Only* file Wadsworth had entrusted to her. Given his violent death, she wasn't sure how to handle it.

******

It was 7:10 pm when Josh entered his apartment by the beach. He spent the day driving to amusement park sites and taking measurements that would help ensure the safety of exciting summer rides.

On the way back, he imagined that Nancy would be waiting for him. As soon as he opened the door, she would greet him wearing only a tee shirt and panties. After several passionate kisses, she would remove her top and panties and lead him to the bed. There, they would make love at least twice before falling into a deep sleep.

Josh opened the door to find nothing but an empty apartment. He walked into the kitchen, removed a beer from the refrigerator, popped the top, and sat on the front porch feeling sorry for himself.

He checked his cell phone for the latest news and found the story of a Princeton professor tortured and beheaded in his home. He was three paragraphs into the article before he realized that Professor Wadsworth was the victim. Apparently, the gas explosion and fire were designed to cover up a gruesome murder.

Understanding the violence surrounding Nancy's story, he called her cell phone, praying she was okay. After five rings, she answered.

"I know. I'm involved in a national story of Middle East terrorism and brutality. If I had any sense, I'd come clean with the authorities and find another topic for my project. But the truth is that I've already invested too much time and effort to look for something new. And, what's more, this story could be my stepping stone to the big time."

Josh tried to provide optimism tempered by his concern for her well-being.

"Look, we've already been through this, and you and I both concluded that you should stay on course while trying to stay safe. But, given this new information, it looks to me like we're dealing with a completely different situation. Your Princeton professor had knowledge of or was involved in a plot that motivated others to use the worst kind of brutality. I don't want you getting in the way of people who would torture and kill for gold, silver, or anything else."

There was a long pause as Nancy thought through her next words.

"Look, I'm sorry that I've burdened you with this. If we hadn't met at Lamberti's, we'd both be on our own, and you wouldn't be concerned. But I can't give up the story, and I can't say goodbye to our love for one another. Now, I need you more than ever."

Trapped, Josh offered his opinion.

"Let me know how I can help. I have Sunday off, and the Camaro is gassed up and ready to go."

"I'm outlining three articles that will tell much of the story. Why don't you drive to Yardley, and we can consult if you know what I mean."

Feeling rejuvenated, Josh responded without delay.

"I'll see you at 10:00 am tomorrow at the house. Have a good sleep."

PART THREE

EYES ONLY

CHAPTER 12

It was 7:30 am, and the streets of this beautiful home of colorful restaurants, inns, and theatres were almost empty. It would be hours before those who hosted the rich and famous would report preparing for another summer Sunday.

Nancy drove her parent's Honda to the two-lane road that led to a picturesque canal that borders the town. On summer days, row boats and canoes frequented the canal that provided a relaxing trip along the calm waters and trees full of green leaves and nesting birds.

The call from Wadsworth's secretary/assistant came at 5:00 am. Carol had to see Nancy at a place that would be private and safe. She refused to discuss the topic but said the information she would provide could be important to the investigation of the Professor's murder.

Nancy left a note for Josh, letting him know that she should be home soon, that she was meeting with someone with information for her story.

She parked the car in a small blacktop lot that bordered the canal. Carol was to meet her there at 8:00 am. Before long, two more cars pulled into the lot, each towing a canoe. It didn't take long for the two drivers and their four children to launch their crafts and paddle away down the waterway.

Nancy began to worry about Carol. Given the level of violence that surrounded the story, there were no limits to the fears that were gripping all those involved. Nancy got out of her car and walked to the edge of the water. It was a peaceful environment, a place where folks came to forget their troubles and enjoy the beauty of nature.

She sat on a wooden bench facing the canal, wondering if she would ever see Carol again. She checked her watch ten minutes after eight. Then, a Kia Sorrento SUV parked in the lot, and Nancy saw Carol get out of her car and walk to the bench.

Nancy studied her new friend as she moved towards her. Carol must have been in her forties, tall and slender. She moved with a certain hesitancy that betrayed the doubts that were attacking her perceived confidence. She sat next to Nancy, and the two hugged.

Carol placed a thick, padded, tan manila envelope in her lap. Nancy was surprised, not spotting it as Carol approached.

The two women faced each other, and Carol began their quiet conversation.

"The Friday before the Professor's murder, he left this envelope with me. He had just received it via Federal Express. The sender was an old acquaintance, an antiquities dealer he knew in Jordan. He asked me to keep it safe over the weekend and said he would take it back on Monday afternoon when he came into the office. It says "Eyes Only" on the label in the upper right-hand corner.

"It may contain the copper scroll and guide that are supposed to offer an easy-to-understand route to the treasure. To be safe, it can only be opened by experts who have equipment that protects material made brittle over thousands of years.

"I was up all night trying to decide what I should do with it. Of course, I could send it to the police investigating the murder. But, if it involves the Professor's research, I'm not sure they would be capable of moving forward with it.

"On the other hand, the Professor said he didn't want to burden President Parnes or any of the staff with these findings.

"And so, those thoughts have led me to you. You

are familiar with the Dead Sea Scrolls, the Professor's research, and the murder investigation. At the same time, you can use a reporter's pledge of confidentiality to withhold the source of the information.

"I have a husband and two young children, and quite simply, I can't get involved."

Nancy wondered what she was getting into. Was this new information so explosive that it led to the Professor's death? If those responsible learned that she now possessed the scroll, would she be next?

It didn't matter. She was a reporter, and she was already into the story. She would use this new information to advance her report and would get it out to the public before desperate men could suppress the findings or kill again.

Nancy looked Carol in the eye.

"You can leave the material with me. I'll not reveal its source. If it's appropriate, I'll use the relevant information included in my story. If the scroll and guide are included, I'll make sure they are protected by experts."

"I can't thank you enough," Carol said.

The two hugged again and drove away in opposite directions.

******

It was nine-thirty when Nancy drove into her parent's driveway. The red Camaro was parked in front of the house.

Josh had read the note left for him at the front door and walked around back. She found him sitting on a deck bench, checking his cellphone emails.

Josh stood, and the two embraced, kissing passionately.

"I know what you want to do, and I do too, but first, I think we need to discuss a new development with my story.

"I just met with an unnamed source who provided me with this envelope. I think we need to sit down and discuss what we should do with it."

Josh put his arms around her again, holding Nancy close.

"I'll do whatever you say. I know your story is important, but I'm not going to see you injured or worse over some ancient treasure that may not even exist."

They kissed again, after which Nancy sat down on one of three benches built into the wooden deck. She looked into his eyes and asked Josh to join her on the bench.

She held up the thick manila envelope.

"Whatever is in here may be the motive behind Dr. Wadsworth's killing. I've agreed to examine it and, if it's relevant, use it in my story. I've also promised to use my reporter's confidentiality to keep its source secret.

"Given the way we feel about each other, I think it would be wise if you were not exposed to the information until it is published. I would never forgive myself if you became another victim of the devils who tortured and then killed the Professor."

Josh took her hand.

"I love you for that, but I don't see how denying the information to me will provide any protection. I'm already involved in your story, and I intend to be by your side regardless. Knowing one piece of the puzzle won't mean anything. If they go after either of us, perhaps the other can offer some assistance."

"I knew you wouldn't agree, but I had to try. Let's go into the kitchen. I'll make the coffee, and we can see what we have."

Each took a sip of the freshly brewed coffee, and Nancy slid a letter opener under the glued flap. She opened the *Eyes-Only* envelope and removed the contents, a few sheets of Professor Wadsworth's stationery and a metal container the size of a textbook, sealed at both ends.

Nancy removed the top sheet and began reading the professor's words aloud.

I'm writing this with the hope that it will provide an explanation if I'm eliminated by criminal sources from the

Middle East or elsewhere.

My recent trip to Jordan was intended to follow a lead to the 64th instruction of the Copper Scroll and its guide. Based upon an abundance of information, the assumption has been that the 64th instruction will open the door to the incredible treasure promised by the other instructions, each identifying the location of valuable minerals and religious objects. Recent estimates put the value of the treasure at two billion dollars in silver, gold, and rare religious ornaments, buried in multiple locations near the site of Jerusalem's Second Temple.

Shortly after I arrived at Amman Jordan's Grand Hyatt, an antiquities dealer who I saved from assault many years ago instructed that I place $2,500 in American dollars into his account in the Bank of Jordan. The next day I received instructions to follow a path into one of Amman's more questionable districts.

My cell phone rang, and I was directed to an outdoor café. Soon, after sitting and ordering two cups of Arabic coffee, my friend, now of advanced years, joined me. He thanked me for the $2,500 and said it was the only payment he will ever receive in connection with the copper scroll.

Then, he told me that a minor quake recently unearthed a sealed vessel that contained a second Copper Scroll. Apparently, his nephew found the container while exploring the caves where the Dead Sea Scrolls, initially discovered by Bedouin shepherds, were located thousands of years ago.

The old man finished his coffee and smiled.

He told me that there are teams of treasure hunters who would purchase the new scroll for hundreds of thousands of dollars. However, he said he had waited decades to find an opportunity to repay my bravery in saving him from the attack of three hoodlums many years ago. And so, he was entrusting the scroll to me.

He cautioned that the scroll is thousands of years old and brittle. His nephew is an archeology student who used special tools to open its container, briefly examine the contents, and re-seal the ancient vessel. He did not have the photographic equipment that would allow the contents to be read without endangering the copper material.

He wanted me to translate the writings of the newly discovered scroll and use them as I saw fit. Given my work in the seminary, he believed that any treasure that resulted would be used to promote peace and assist those in need.

Then, he warned that there may be some danger in this undertaking. There are those who are selling treasure maps that pretend to represent the guide of the 64th instruction. If the newly discovered scroll is used to retrieve the hidden items, these efforts will put such charlatans out of business.

Also, he said that in recent years, given that no treasure has ever been recovered, there is a growing belief by some that the Copper Scroll and its treasure, including the guide of the 64th instruction, has always been nothing but *a scam.*

According to this account, when it appeared that the Second Temple could be destroyed by the Romans, a small sect in Jerusalem invested in preparing the Copper Scroll. After the invasion, it was used to lead the Romans and others seeking a quick fortune in the wrong direction. When it was concluded that the information was phony, the Scroll was hidden in the remote caves near Khirbet Qumran, away from Jerusalem.

This newly discovered scroll could provide more phony leads or might actually furnish a path to a treasure worth billions of dollars. Apparently, in addition to a narrative, the scroll includes a map that could lead to a single location.

I have decided to accept this challenge, Helping to Discover the Copper Scroll treasure, if it exists. This could be the crowning achievement of my seminary research.

However, if someone else is reading this before I begin my new work, I must assume that I have been killed by those with divergent interests. In that case, all I ask is that you use your best judgement to fulfill the wishes of my Jordanian friend, who will remain nameless in the interest of his security.

God bless.

Nancy reacted with no delay.

"So, if Wadsworth's narrative is to be believed,

as I suspected, the copper scroll sought for thousands of years was phony. It was designed to lead the Romans away from the treasure. If this newly discovered scroll is legitimate, it could provide directions to the treasure."

CHAPTER 13

Josh and Nancy spent Sunday brainstorming how they might react to this new development. Josh kicked off the speculation.

"Okay, we could provide the new scroll directly to the Israeli Antiquities Department, explaining how it was obtained and the price that was paid with Professor Wadsworth's life. It wouldn't be sexy, but it would get the job done, providing a closing chapter to your article. And it would relieve us of the danger of possessing the scroll.

"At the other extreme, we could partner with someone who has the equipment and expertise to open the container, read the scroll, and follow the map and narrative information to the treasure. Of course, that would violate the terms accepted by the Professor. At the same time, our efforts would cease to be in the interest of a story in favor of gaining personal wealth."

Nancy interrupted.

"I'm beginning to see a third way that would juice up my story while maintaining the Professor's intentions. In my three articles, we use the Professor's words to describe how he obtained the new scroll, how it was intended to be used, and how it led to his death. Then, on live TV, we display the container, revealing the new copper scroll and presenting it to a representative of the Israeli Antiquities Department. As part of the deal, if the scroll becomes the foundation of an expedition to retrieve the Temple's treasure, I receive exclusive rights to cover the story."

"I think that's got it all, except for one thing," Josh responded. "We need to place the scroll in a safety deposit box and take steps to stay safe ourselves. Remember, they killed the Professor once they were convinced that he didn't have the scroll. His beheading is a warning to others not to play games with possession of the scroll."

"Okay," Nancy responded, "as soon as my parents arrive home, we'll make a very interesting deposit."

Wanting to keep the momentum going, they described a three-part series designed to captivate the nation.

She would begin with the brutal murder of

Professor Wadsworth, who he was, and why he was tortured and killed. Nancy would highlight her being the only witness to the explosion and fire that destroyed the Professor's home. A picture of what's left of the house would document the force of the explosion.

The second installment would offer a history of the Dead Sea Scrolls and more specifically, the copper scroll and the guide of the sixty-fourth instruction. The piece would recount how they have been a powerful magnet to treasure hunters, and their extensive efforts to find and possess huge amounts of gold and silver promised.

The unique information retrieved by the Professor in Jordan, including the second copper scroll, would be the blockbuster reserved for the third article. It would be presented live on air to an Israeli representative of its Antiquities Department. Nancy would furnish popular speculation of where the treasure could be hiding and promise to add to her series of articles after the Israelis translated information on the new scroll and either planned to follow its course to the treasure or rejected its contents as irrelevant.

Once the articles and accompanying scripts were in draft, she would send them via e-mail to her mentor, Professor Harold Carr, who was spending the summer in Jordan. She would seek his editorial assistance as well as advice regarding respected publications/

TV affiliates that might be interested in acquiring/ releasing the series. His ties to the Philadelphia Inquirer and Philadelphia's ABC affiliate were well known, and Nancy believed he might convince their editorial staff to publish/broadcast the material.

******

Monday morning marked the end of Nancy and Josh's living together as though they were a married couple. They slept in, made love, and went out for breakfast at the Ewing Diner. Later that day, around dinner time, Nancy's parents would be home from their vacation at the Greenbrier.

Josh left for the shore in mid-afternoon while Nancy went to the supermarket to restock the kitchen for her mother. If experience ruled, her folks would rave about the meals and golf at the resort. However, they would be tired from all the activities and need rest over the next few days.

Being an only child, Nancy was very close to her parents. From her birth, both mother and father fussed over all her accomplishments, whether it was walking before she was a year old or her entrance and fine grades at Drexel.

Her dad was semi-retired from a promotions firm he founded, while her mother focused on weekly bridge games and raising funds for a local hospital. Both were avid golfers, participating in leagues sponsored by the Yardley Country Club.

Nancy checked her watch. It was 6:00 pm. Expecting her folks by dinner time, she called her mom's cell phone to check on their progress. They were thirty minutes from home.

******

On Tuesday morning, Nancy borrowed the key to her parent's safety deposit box and secured the new scroll. She began three days of working almost around the clock. The race was on. Could she put it all together as a polished series of articles that would form the basis of an hour-long TV special before those seeking the information learned what she was up to? If they were unaware of the existence of the *Eyes-Only* file and second copper scroll, Carol figured there was a good chance she'd make it.

One positive development was the return of her Drexel mentor from the Middle East. With the first draft of her work in hand, she drove to Philadelphia, parked in a student lot, and walked into the modern building that housed Communications and Journalism.

Professor Carr was celebrating his fifteenth year at Drexel. He was a big man, over six feet tall and close to two-hundred and fifty pounds, with dark eyes and a thick black mustache. Nancy knocked on his closed door, hoping he hadn't been called away from their scheduled meeting.

"If it's Ms. Troll, come on in."

Nancy opened the door and entered. Given the time he spent away, his office was loaded with all kinds of mail and unanswered notices.

"It's going to take me a week just to catch up with my mail," he said.

"Now, what's the state of your senior project?"

Carr put a pile of letters aside and looked into Nancy's eyes.

Nancy began with a brief review of the copper scroll's anticipated content. Then, she recreated her first-hand experience witnessing Professor Wadsworth's murder. Finally, she relayed the material in the *Eyes-Only* package, not identifying how she received it.

"So, your project will tell this rather fantastic story? How do we know that the new scroll will add anything substantial? Given that no one has ever found anything of value using the original copper scroll as a guide, the new scroll may be another dud. Also, are we sure that the killing of Wadsworth was related to any of this? From what I've heard, the police have yet to arrest anyone for Wadsworth's murder."

Nancy took a deep breath and organized her thoughts. She knew Carr would be skeptical. In fact, she valued his criticism to tighten her presentation for others who would be looking to punch holes in her conclusions.

"I think, once you read the proposed articles, you may feel differently. But let me take your objections one at a time and see if I can help.

"First, the police found that Wadsworth was tied to a chair and tortured before he was beheaded. Two or three men must have been involved in his questioning and murder and in the house explosion. Considering Wadsworth's recent trip to Jordan and the way in which he was killed, linking all this to his work on the treasure doesn't appear to be a stretch.

"Second, it is true that no one has ever found any of the treasure. But, according to the first scroll, the guide of the sixty-fourth instruction will open the door to accurate directions to the gold and silver promised. The second copper scroll may be that guide.

"Given that it, too, is thousands of years old and brittle, I have placed it in my parents' safety deposit box, undisturbed within its container. It may well give us what's needed to find the treasure. Certainly, having this information would be a reasonable motive for Wadsworth's questioning and murder.

"Finally, there have been added indications that men are continuing to search for the information Wadsworth received. After my interview with Wadsworth, my parents' house was broken into and searched. A house I visited in Ocean City was also ransacked. I spotted the man involved in these break-ins at the memorial service for the Professor."

Nancy, looking into her mentor's eyes, detected a new seriousness in his attitude.

"Okay, Nancy, give me a day or so to read through the articles. I'll provide editing and raise questions that need to be addressed. While I'm reviewing the written content, you need to list the visual inserts we'll need for a TV special if one is scheduled.

"Given the violence of the surrounding circumstances, we need to get the series published as soon as possible. Then, we'll work to find a TV outlet willing to present your findings on air, along with any updated information."

CHAPTER 14
YEAR 70 AD
JERUSALEM

They sat around an ornate table in the administrative wing of the Second Temple. The Temple Treasurer, leader of the House of Hakkov, had summoned the military, spiritual, and commercial leaders to an emergency session. There was fear in the air as each man knew, in their hearts, that the end was coming. Scouts had spotted the Roman army preparing for invasion. No defense could repel the death and destruction that was coming.

Emanuel Hakkov was dressed in a fine linen garment covered by a colorful shawl, with tassels attached to the corners as reminders to keep the Lord's commandments. A rose-colored turban reinforced his high status among the elders. Dark rings under his eyes were a testament to the many nights spent trying to prepare for the invaders. He rose and addressed the group.

"I am not denying the skills of our army or the potency of the prayers being offered to spare us the wrath of the Romans. But I can't, in good faith, sit by while the days evaporate like smoke and no steps are taken to save our majestic temple from Roman plunder.

"My advisors and I have devised a plan to save our most precious religious and financial assets from Roman hands. This will require your support and sacrifices. It is a plan of two parts and so before you react, please allow us to complete our presentation.

"First, we must spend the next week, days and nights, assembling our most holy religious ornaments, gold, silver, and rare stones. They would be brought to the lot, where we ask pilgrims to wait before entering the holy temple. I have bought many carts, wagons, and draft animals to accommodate the resources that will be denied to the invaders.

"Second, a caravan will be formed to transport our valuables from the temple to a secure location many millins away. The content will be disguised as construction materials removed from recently renovated rooms in the Temple's basement.

"My men have developed a map that will allow our route to avoid the area's many difficult natural obstacles while taking advantage of wells for the sustenance of our animals.

"While the caravan exits the area, I have contracted with expert scribes to develop a copper scroll that will lead the Romans on a futile search for the very assets that will be safely transported away. A draft of the scroll talks about sixty-four locations and a valuable guide that will identify where our gold, silver, and most valuable religious mementos may be found. Whoever follows that scroll and its guide will find nothing but frustration."

The High Priest, dressed in a loosely fitting black and white robe that extended over his head as a yarmulke, rose to respond.

"I don't care about the gold, silver, and jewels that could provide for material gain. But our temple cannot function without the menorahs and sacred lamps that signify the Lord's caring. We should never separate those heavenly gifts from the Temple for which they were intended."

Hakkov turned to face the religious and moral leader of the Jewish people.

"My friend, the question isn't if our holy artifacts are to be separated from the Temple but rather who is to possess them after the invasion. If we leave them as is, the Romans will take them from us and desecrate their being. If you approve our plan, we will remove them for safe keeping, to be retrieved when we can rebuild the Temple."

The Priest wasn't through.

"The walls of Jerusalem will withstand the Roman attempt to capture the Temple. Our Zealots will repel any efforts to denigrate the Lord's House."

"I appreciate your confidence in our forces," Hakkov responded. "But the Romans rarely are denied their targets. Recent conquests have seen them throw burning torches over fortress walls to consume all those within.

"If we remove the gold, silver, and artifacts for safekeeping, and the Romans leave the Temple alone, I will be the first to organize a caravan to return our holy belongings to their rightful place."

The Rabbi called his closest advisors to him. They followed into his residence, closing the door behind them. Hakkov and the rest of the Temple's seniors waited for the questions to come.

An hour later, the Rabbi and his men returned. Hakkov hoped they were coming to their senses.

The Rabbi invited Hakkov and his troop into his private residence. They sat around a polished wooden table with a gold menorah in the middle.

The Rabbi began the interrogation.

"I know you are an honorable person and that your intentions are with God. However, we have a few key questions that must be answered before we can decide the fate of the temple's valuables.

"First, where would you take our assets, and how will they be both hidden and preserved?"

Hakkov glanced at Ethan Glazer, his first deputy. A look of satisfaction passed between the two, recognizing that all the work they did on their own may have been worth it.

"As I think you know, there is a Great Salt Sea just three days from the temple. We have thoroughly explored the shoreline and discovered a deep fissure lined with a solid layer of tar. The caravan will unload its gold and silver into the bottom of the space. Then, our heavenly relics will be wrapped and stored on top.

"I have contracted with skilled workers to construct a cover to tightly fit over the storage unit. It is made of dark wood to be sealed with tar retrieved from the sea's shoreline. Finally, the cover will be buried by a layer of salty soil common to the area."

Although impressed, the Rabbi had more questions.

"I know that the region you have targeted is not well populated. But how will you ensure that others will not follow the caravan, see the treasure being secured, and steal its contents once the caravan leaves?"

Hakkov was ready with his response.

"Rabbi, the caravan will be led by seniors who present no threat to those it may encounter. There will be no hint of the treasure being transported. A contingent of troops, disguised as holy men, will camp near the final location to ensure that the site has not been compromised. These men, Sicarii rebels, have been recruited from the Masada fortification near the Sea."

"If many years pass before we are able to rebuild our temple, how will the location of our treasure be found?"

"We have drafted instructions and a map that pinpoints the estimated location where the valuables will be deposited. The map will be amended based upon the actual journey. When finalized, a second copper scroll will document the location of our treasures to be passed-on from generation to generation, if it must be."

Impressed with the information provided, the Rabbi allowed the plan to proceed.

CHAPTER 15

The blast flattened the Troll residence, killing Nancy's parents and destroying copies of the articles and TV feature she had prepared. The originals were in her possession as she drove to Philadelphia to meet with one of the Inquirer's feature editors. If it weren't for a last-minute change of the meeting time, moving it up an hour, she would have perished in the explosion as well.

When she entered the newspaper's building before she could ask the location of the office in which she was to meet, an elderly man with styled grey hair and sympathetic eyes approached.

"Are you Nancy Troll?" he asked.

Initially pleased with her reception, she answered "yes," figuring that her mentor's advance work likely captured the interest of the paper.

"Please follow me," he said.

Nancy began to sense that something was wrong when the man led her to the office of the paper's editor-in-chief.

"I thought we were meeting with Bob Hurely, one of your feature editors," she said.

"Please come in and sit down," he responded.

"I'm Ralph Hamel, the Inquirer's Editor-In-Chief. I'm afraid I have bad news. A few minutes ago, we received an AP report that a home in Yardley had been destroyed by an explosion. From what we can tell, it's your house that was targeted."

Nancy couldn't breathe. What had she done? Now, her drive for fame as a reporter resulted in the death of her parents.

"Did my parents survive?" she asked.

"The report said there were no survivors."

She shifted in her chair, bending over, resting her elbows on her knees. Her mind flashed back to the explosion at Professor Wadsworth's home. Questions shot through her consciousness.

Did they torture her mother and father before destroying the house? Were they alive when the blast occurred? Did they suffer through the fire?

Her mind turned back to the scheduled meeting.

"Has Professor Carr arrived for our meeting?" she asked.

Hamel poured a glass of water for each of them.

"Please, let's try to calm down and think through this," he said.

Nancy ignored his advice.

"What about Professor Carr?" she persisted.

"We're trying to reach him."

"Did he provide you with drafts of my materials?"

"No, although after my conversation with him over the phone, I have to admit we are very interested."

Nancy stood up, trying to get her bearings.

"I'm sorry, but I can't stay here."

Hamel rose from his chair and reached out, holding Nancy's hand, looking into her eyes.

"I know this is difficult, but you are in shock and need to wait. I've talked with the authorities and a team should be here any minute. Please, sit back down."

Nancy had to get out into the fresh air. She grabbed the backpack that contained her originals, thanked Hamels for his concern, and rushed out the door. Once outside, she took a deep breath and walked to her car, two blocks from the Inquirer. Parked in a metered spot, she sat behind the wheel, trying to gather her thoughts.

She pulled her cell phone from her purse and dialed Professor Carr's office. The phone rang four times, then his secretary picked-up.

"Professor Carr's office, may I help you?"

It took more than a few seconds before the words left Nancy's mouth.

"I'm sorry. This is Nancy Troll. Is the professor in?"

There was a delay in response as the secretary checked her supervisor's schedule.

"Ms. Troll, the Professor left for your meeting a half hour ago. Has he not arrived?"

Nancy's mind raced, trying to make logical choices.

"If he returns, please ask him to call my cell. He has the number."

Nancy ended the call and dialed the professor's cell directly, praying that he would pick up. But the phone rang eight times, activating a scripted message advising that he was unavailable.

She pictured Professor Wadsworth's headless body tied to a chair. Then, a vision of her parents suffering the same fate invaded her mind.

Unable to catch her breath, she bent over, her head between her knees, fighting to gain control. Her heart raced.

A tapping on the driver's side window brought panic. Fearing what she would find, she sat up slowly and looked.

A uniformed police officer motioned for her to lower the window.

"Ma'am, are you alright? Are you in some kind of trouble?"

The policeman must have been a rookie cop, still in his twenties. He had a white complexion, dark brown eyes, and a look of honest concern.

Nancy started the car and lowered her window.

"Thank you, officer, I'm okay. I just received some difficult news from the university."

"Well, you hang in there," he said, turning and walking away.

She had one more call to make. Did her ambition also kill the love of her life?

If Professor Carr had been accounted for, she figured that the assassins may have limited their scheme to her and her family. With the Professor missing, she feared for Josh's life, too.

It was early on a weekday morning, and he should have been at work. She dialed his cell. When the phone went to its programmed message, she hung up, thinking the worst.

Nancy was alone, the target of Middle East assassins. An unscheduled change in the start time of a meeting saved her life. She couldn't count on another random event to keep her alive. When the assassins discover that she was not in her parents' house, they would be after her, seeking to destroy the documentation that might undermine their schemes or, on a positive note, find new information that could lead them to the treasure.

Her mind examined how she might survive. Could the police keep her safe, or should she run and hide?

Before she could decide, her cell phone rang. She picked-up, seeing that it was Josh.

"Are you okay?" she asked.

"I was at work. On a break, I saw that you were trying to reach me. How is it going? Did you meet with the newspaper this morning?"

Nancy unloaded on the man she loved.

"My parents are dead, and Professor Carr is missing. When they find out that I wasn't in the house when it exploded, they'll find me and kill me, too."

Josh sensed Nancy's panic. He had to calm her down and devise a strategy for their survival.

"Okay, try to go through the chronology of events."

Nancy took a deep breath and explained what had happened.

CHAPTER 16
MONDAY, AUGUST 12, 2019
TRENTON, NEW JERSEY

The single-family house on Trenton's West State Street had been empty since August 1. That was when Josh's Aunt Helen left for her annual month's stay at the Jersey Shore near Point Pleasant. The house was seventy-five feet from the street with a stand-alone two-car garage located next to the back yard. Blocks of similar homes on both sides of the street covered the landscape as far as the eye could see.

With his parents both deceased, during most of the year, Josh rented a small apartment near the Stockton campus. In the summer, if he was lucky, he found a place near the beach, like the Ocean City rental he reserved until the end of August.

He had a key to his aunt's home from the days when she suggested that he use the residence as a quiet place in which he could prepare papers required for university assignments. She was a widow and appreciated his company any time.

Since he might also be a target, Josh told Nancy to meet him at the West State Street address. It would be their safehouse until they had a chance to devise a comprehensive approach to solve their dilemma.

He got a week's worth of groceries while still in Ocean City. Then, he drove the Camaro to Trenton and into his aunt's garage. The daily paper had been canceled, and Josh would make sure they didn't use the lights in the front of the house. If his strategy was effective, the neighbors and others in the area would conclude that the house continued to be empty.

******

Before leaving for their hideaway, Nancy drove by what was left of her parents' home. She knew it was foolish, but she had to see it for herself. Parked nearby, memories of her wonderful childhood rushed into her mind. She owed it all to the mother and father who lost their lives to her obsession for professional recognition. She wasn't sure if she would be able to live with herself.

She followed Google Maps directions from Yardley to the house on West State Street in Trenton. Close to an hour later, Josh spotted her pulling into the driveway. He directed her to park the Honda in the garage next to the Camaro. After he closed the garage door, she joined him on the small, cement back porch.

He put his arms around her, holding her tightly.

"You must believe that we will get through this. I know you feel guilty but there was no way you could have predicted this outcome. It wasn't your fault.

"From my perspective, your enthusiasm to publish the truth about the treasure should eventually save lives. Your articles will expose the devils responsible for violence and lead the police to their identity and location."

Nancy looked into Josh's bright blue eyes, feeling gratitude for his words, even though she was skeptical of their veracity.

She took his hand and led him into the house and up the stairs. She walked them into a back bedroom, closed the door, and removed her top, throwing her blouse and bra onto the floor. Then, she placed his hands on her breasts. She sighed as he lightly circled her nipples with his thumbs.

When she couldn't resist any longer, she moved him on to the bed. They stripped off their remaining clothes and crawled under the top sheet.

She wanted him to make rough love, relegating her to an object only interested in pleasure from a superior being. She didn't want to think about anything, just to build towards a climax that would take over her world, release her from blame.

After a few seconds, Josh got the message. Her sweet face and eyes demanded that he use force, deeper and deeper, creating a craving that could not be denied. When her release finally came, she burst into tears, a child who had lost the parents she loved, a woman who had found the man she would adore forever.

Half asleep, Nancy turned her head to look into Josh's eyes.

"At least the second copper scroll is safe."

When they woke, he removed the batteries from their cellphones, making sure the devices didn't lead the killers to them.

*****

Harold Carr collapsed on the cabin's single bed and tried to steady his nerves. It had been an experience from a Jason Bourne thriller. He loved the adventure and unpredictable content of today's stories of suspense but had no desire to live in one.

His borrowed clothes were damp, not taking the time to shower and dry off. A chill shot through his body. It was August in the Pocono Mountains, and the nights could be quite cold. Before trying to fall asleep, he reviewed the fantastic events that led him there.

He left his house near the Cobb Creek Golf Course in Ardmore at 7:30 am, heading for the Philly Grill, where he would greet the neighborhood buddies he hadn't seen since returning from Jordan. They'd recount their summer experiences, speculate on the coming football season of their Eagles, and make a date for golf. Then, he'd join Ms. Troll at the Inquirer and help to promote her article and TV spot.

Heading down Millburne Road to Chestnut, he spotted a silver Mercedes following too close. He sped up, but the car stayed near his bumper.

His mind flashed back to Professor Wadsworth and the violence described in Troll's article. Instantly, he downshifted and floored the accelerator. The turbo kicked in, and his red Hyundai Veloster took off, leaving the Mercedes far behind.

With his rearview mirror clear, he slowed to the 35 mile per hour posted speed and began to relax. Then, out of nowhere, a drone crashed into his windshield, breaking the glass and making it impossible to see what was ahead. He slammed on the brakes. Just as the sports car came to a halt, a pick-up truck struck from the side, pushing the vehicle off the road, onto a field, and then into a pond.

With the air intake blocked, the engine died, and pond water sprayed through the cracked windshield and in through the door jams. Panic struck, and Carr froze, realizing that the vehicle had landed on its side. His only alternative was to somehow try to open the passenger side door and swim up to the surface. With the water of the pond against it, he wasn't sure if he would have the strength necessary.

He unlatched his seatbelt and tried to maneuver across the driver's front seat to the door, avoiding the console and its stick shift. It was an uphill battle made even more difficult by the water that was rising fast. In two or three minutes, the car would be filled with pond water, and he would be through.

Then, it dawned on him. There was no need to open the door if he could gradually lower the window. He reached back to the steering wheel console, praying that battery-powered commands were still functioning. He clicked to open the door locks, took a deep breath, and slowly retracted the passenger side window.

As the water rushed in, he held on to the steering wheel. With the body of the car mostly full, he took a deep breath and got into position. Placing his feet against the center console, he propelled himself through the open window and out into the pond.

Despite the summer heat, the water felt cold, and his slacks and shirt clung to his body, making it difficult to move. Luckily, a bright sun shone into the pond, allowing Carr to follow it up and into the fresh morning air.

He didn't know if they'd be waiting for him or just assumed that they had done their dirty work and left the scene of the crime. He made his way to the edge of the water and lifted himself out and onto the ground. He stretched out, exhausted, waiting for his breathing to become normal and his heart to stop pounding. The assailants were nowhere to be seen.

After several minutes, he was able to stand and make his way to the edge of the road. As luck would have it, one of his buddies, heading to the Philly Diner, spotted him, slammed on his brakes, and picked him up. After a rushed explanation, his friend agreed to loan him their teen's car and some dry clothes.

Carr needed to disappear and develop a strategy to stay alive. He didn't know if his student survived. With his cellphone at the bottom of the pond, easy communications were prohibited. Driving the borrowed car, he would head for the Poconos and a rarely used cabin owned by his former wife's family.

PART FOUR

WHO DO YOU TRUST?

CHAPTER 17
WEDNESDAY, AUGUST 14, 2019
YARDLEY, PENNSYLVANIA

No less than thirty police cars were parked around the branch of the First American Bank in Yardley's Suburban Shopping Center. When Aaron Ausmus, the bank manager, pulled into his parking space at 6:30 am, he couldn't believe his eyes. The six e-CAM security cameras guaranteed to spot any irregularities had been disabled, their lenses smashed into a thousand pieces, glass scattered around the parking lot.

And yet, there had been no alarm, no official notice that something was wrong.

Afraid to approach the bank, he called their security coordinator who had a puzzling response.

"What's the problem, Aaron?"

"That's a hell of a question," Ausmus said, contempt in his voice. "You mean to tell me you're unaware that all our security cameras have been shot to pieces! You better get your ass down here because I'm not going to enter the facility not knowing what I'll find."

When e-CAM's security chief for the region and a captain from the Yardley Police Force approached the bank's main door, they found it unlocked and opened a crack. The office that held customer records had been ransacked, and the vault door had been blown open by an explosive device.

Since several deposit boxes had been broken into, it was impossible to tell which had been the target of this daring robbery. The bank's cash reserves were untouched.

After a thorough investigation of the situation, the company's security chief concluded that someone had hacked into the bank's security system, blocking any awareness of the attack.

"We're going to have to close each branch until we identify the process used and construct new safeguards," he said.

******

Three men of Arab descent sat around a box that rested on a table of polished cedar. The container, made of dark, heavy metal, was rectangular, twelve inches long, six inches wide, and eight inches thick. One of the men, a Middle East antiquities expert, carefully lifted the tab that held the container shut. He pushed it in front of their leader, in his thirties with a full, closely cut beard. He addressed his two partners.

"This provides directions to billions in gold, silver, and temple valuables. I've studied the procedures used to guard against copper scroll degeneration. We'll position it gently and take pictures that will allow us to fully examine its contents without damaging the original document. Since we've eliminated others searching for the new scroll, we can return to the Middle East with ease and organize our search and recovery mission."

He looked his two partners in the eye.

"This will make all our efforts worthwhile," he said, as he pulled back the overlap, revealing what was inside the metal container.

His face fell, recognizing that the box was empty.

CHAPTER 18
THURSDAY, AUGUST 15, 2019
TRENTON, NEW JERSEY

Commander Auburn and Detectives Moore and Statelmyer cleared security and took an elevator up to the seventh-floor conference room. Their investigation of Professor Wadsworth's murder had gone nowhere.

At first, with no related crimes happening, there was the hope that the murder was a one and done. Somehow, the Professor came into the possession of a piece of information that drew threats from men of violence. Unable to unearth what he was hiding, they did him in and went on to other items of interest out of their jurisdiction. It was, the police hoped, an oddball homicide that would defy investigation and fade in the public's memory.

Then, August 12 happened. The home of the young lady who witnessed Professor Wadsworth's house explosion saw her own house, and her parents meet the same fate. If it hadn't been for a last-minute time change in a meeting between her and an editor of the Philadelphia Inquirer, she would have been in the targeted house. Efforts to find, question, and protect her had been unsuccessful.

At the same time, the woman's college graduate mentor, Harold Carr, who was scheduled to meet with her and an Inquirer editor, had also disappeared. A terrified grammar school student waiting for his bus provided the local police with an account of drones and an attacking truck pushing a car into a nearby pond. When divers investigated, they found Carr's vehicle and cellphone but no Carr.

The police weren't certain if the bank robbery of the 14th was related, but it added to the impression that the area was under attack while the authorities remained in the dark. A page-one article in the Inquirer recounted the chaos and added suspicions that all this was about secret information concerning an ancient Middle East treasure.

Before the New Jersey police officers could take a seat at the long conference table centered in the room, three more officers, two men and a woman, entered. The woman, who looked like she belonged on a movie set, took the floor.

"Gentleman, I am Joan MacLennan, Regional Chief of the Federal Bureau, and this is my Deputy,

Harry Roper. Please take a seat and introduce yourselves."

Commander Auburn introduced the New Jersey contingent. Then, the man who happened to enter with the FBI force, the lone Pennsylvania officer, took the floor.

"As soon as we can take a break from investigating the house explosion and bank robbery, two more officers will be assigned liaison. In the meantime, I am Alvin Harrison, and I'll be coordinating with you all."

The FBI Regional Chief, sitting at the end of the table, took charge. That she would be articulate and well organized was no surprise. What did put the men back was her beautiful face, deep brown eyes, full lips, and slender nose. While she dressed conservatively in a white blouse, black slacks, and jacket, the lines of her full breasts and firm hips could not be disguised.

"Gentlemen, I'd like us to begin by exploring two key questions. First, are the two house explosions, bank robbery, and disappearances of Nancy Troll and Harold Carr all related? And second, if they are related, what is the issue that is driving the violence?"

Auburn spoke up with no delay.

"The MOs of the two house explosions are dissimilar, but the results were the same. Also, the disappearances of Nancy Troll, Harold Carr, and Josh

Rosenberg appear to be related to the subject matter that was to appear in the Inquirer. The bank robbery is suspicious, given that some deposit boxes were robbed while three hundred thousand dollars in cash was left undisturbed. So, we believe it is no stretch to conclude that all this flows from the same issue."

MacLennan looked into Auburn's eyes with intensity.

"And that issue is what?"

"Well, I wish I could be certain about that. Based upon our conversations with personnel at the Princeton Seminary and with Nancy Troll before she disappeared, all of this revolves around an ancient Middle East treasure, where it is, whether it is real or phony, and how much it is worth in today's money. If you agree, maybe we should bring a Middle East antiquities expert on board to provide relevant guidance."

"Okay, let's see if I can advance things a bit?" MacLennan said.

"First, while the results of the two house explosions were similar, the precipitating events were dissimilar. The Princeton explosion was generated from within as a fire spread to a gas leak. On the other hand, the Yardley explosion appears to have been caused by a bomb delivered by an armed drone or missile.

"We do agree that all of this is tied together by the issue of the supposed treasure. However, like you, we're not sure exactly what that means. Is this a treasure whose location is the primary interest, or are the parties trying to suppress information that would unmask the treasure as a hoax? We just don't know.

"We intend to track down the source of the drone or missile that destroyed the Yardley house and the truck that attacked Professor Carr's automobile. Also, I like the idea of bringing a Middle East expert on board, so we'll be working on that."

Auburn spoke up.

"Well, we're going to re-question Seminary and related staff and others who might provide useful input."

MacLennan turned to the Pennsylvania representative, Alvin Harrison, for his view. He was a heavyset man with a dark mustache and balding palate.

"To be honest, we're doing more basic investigative work on the house explosion and disappearances. Perhaps the FBI could share the drone/missile data so we might help."

"Of course," MacLellan responded.

"Why don't you get together with Harry, my Deputy, after we adjourn and make the arrangements? I'm suggesting that we all meet every three days, if not in person, then via computer and Zoom. If we need to talk before that, I have a list of email addresses and telephone numbers to notify you."

Before adjourning, Auburn raised another issue.

"It seems to me that we need to dedicate more resources to find our missing principals. My guess is if the perpetrators find them first, they will not survive."

MacLellan responded.

"I agree. We have designated each as a missing person. A team will be organized later today to search for them. We'll keep you posted on their progress as developments warrant.

"If there are no other issues, let's adjourn. Be sure to let me know of any new occurrences we should investigate.

"Thanks."

As their meeting adjourned, the participants recognized Joan MacLennan as a fast-rising star within the FBI. Her reputation was built on an ability to analyze criminal activity with unprecedented speed and understanding. Her recommendations solved three high visibility cases, preventing death and destruction that were certain to descend on the Mideast Region. These accomplishments led to her promotion as a Regional Chief. Her beauty, while initially offsetting for many, was overlooked as her brilliance and confident leadership became clear.

CHAPTER 19
YEAR 70 AD
JERUSALEM

The night was cold. Strong winds and a negative directive kept pilgrims from the temple, waiting for a more receptive environment. Below, in the area cleared to organize and launch the caravan, selected volunteers worked to disguise the valuables to be saved from the Romans. All the rare stones, ingots of gold and silver, and temple religious ornaments were there.

The gold and silver lined the bottoms of twenty-three wooden carts. The stones and temple religious valuables, individually wrapped, covered the minerals. Finally, strips of cloth and various light building materials and clothing topped off the contents, covering what was below. Each cart was hooked-up to two oxen, animals with the strength to make the difficult journey to the site near the Dead Sea.

When all the carts were ready, the Rabbi

addressed the group.

"My friends, the future of our Temple is in your hands. If the Romans had their way, no physical sign of our faith would survive their attack. The bravery you are displaying will preserve the symbols of our belief in the one God. When doubts invade our minds, the products of your efforts will remind us that we are able to go on in the light of Jewish tradition.

"Before the first Temple was destroyed by the Babylonians, some of the holiest of our possessions were cut into many small pieces to avoid their being captured. Many years ago, my mentor blessed me with what he claimed to be a small piece of Aaron's rod."

The Rabbi held up a six-inch piece of polished dark wood.

"This source of many miracles was removed from the Ark of the Covenant and divided for distribution to those who would rebuild the Temple and maintain our faith. Place this holy object in the lead cart and then on top of the valuables being hidden. It will keep evil from our legacy."

Adam Levi, foreman of Emanuel Hakkov's agricultural ventures, was designated leader of the caravan and worked to secure the temple's valuables. In his younger days, he was a disciplined soldier who rose quickly in the ranks of Jerusalem's defenders. When he reached more mature years, he was rewarded by Hakkov and brought in to work on his estate. Still physically imposing at six feet and two-hundred pounds, he was a leader of men, clever and forceful when the circumstances demanded.

Each cart was driven by men of advanced years. If the Romans discovered the procession, there would be no appearance of a military mission. In fact, the men carried no weapons. From all appearances, this was a peaceful mission to dispose of unwanted materials.

The first day's passage would be the easiest. Well-used roads and trails, some tree-lined, presented favorable conditions for the oxen. Levi led the procession. From time to time, on horseback, he rode from front to back, inspecting each cart and the conditions of the oxen. Containers of fresh water were included to combat the coming heat as they descended into the Judean Desert.

After several hours, Adam rode ahead, looking for the clearing he scouted to accommodate their first night's stay. There was a spring to rejuvenate the animals and level ground to encourage their rest. He was relieved to find the area abandoned. With no delay, he returned to his men, giving them the good news.

"Just around this next corner, a field and spring are waiting to accommodate our first stop. As we discussed previously, we will unhitch and feed the oxen, secure them, and pitch tents for our sleep. Let me know of any problems you meet."

******

Four hours later, with the men and animals fed, final preparations were being made for the night's sleep. Eight hours' rest would provide the energy needed to carry out the demanding journey of the next day.

Out of nowhere, a bolt of lightning woke men and beasts, destroying the confidence that was beginning to build. The winter weather had been unusually dry and calm. When they entered the Judean desert, it was a barren expanse of sand, yellow and gold in color, with dry gullies and calm ravines dominating the landscape. All that was about to change as enormous downpours fell from the sky.

Adam Levi's worst nightmare was upon him. He addressed the men.

"We must move to higher ground, secure the oxen, and wait out the storm. When it subsides, we will find a new route to the Dead Sea and our destination."

Before he could reorganize his caravan, the flat land on which the men and oxen had settled was surrounded by surging water rushing down two separate wadis. One cart and its two oxen, ahead of the others, set out for higher ground but got caught in the torrent within one of the numerous gullies. The two animals, thrown on their backs, disappeared around a bend. The cart sailed through the racing waters as though it was designed for aquatic maneuvers.

The old man in charge of that cart was unable to hold the reins. The momentum created by the waters saw him hit the ground and slide just over the edge and into the gully.

Levi ran to his aid, grabbing him by his collar as he was about to be taken by the rising stream. Two of the remaining men grabbed Levi's legs, keeping him from the gusher.

As he was about to pull the submerged man out of the stream, a loose boulder crashed into Levi's head, killing him instantly. In shock, the men behind let Levi and the other man go. Their bodies disappeared under the water and around the bend.

CHAPTER 20

FRIDAY, AUGUST 16, 2019
PRINCETON, NEW JERSEY

Carol Stark sat quietly in her husband's den. He was on a three-week business trip. Her hope was to sell the newly discovered scroll she appropriated from the "Eyes Only" package given to her by Director Wadsworth before her husband's return.

Although their family life appeared ideal, the truth was very different. Her husband of twelve years had a serious addiction to gambling on sports. Occasionally, he would hit it big, and she would find herself on a luxurious vacation. But over the long run, he was building a huge debt from which they would never recover.

While this was a problem of many years, she blamed the depth of their dilemma on the 2018 Supreme Court decision that gave birth to new websites that made it easy and legal to wager on sports, much of it televised.

In terms of mental and emotional impact, her husband's sickness was comparable to being hooked on drugs. And while there was a general recognition of the growing problem with sports betting, little guidance was offered to those with the addiction.

At the source of the problem was his belief that his own ability to know how sporting events would end was at such a high level that it would pay enormous dividends. Instead, his betting spent the equity in their home and created three mortgages.

When the Professor was killed, Carol couldn't resist opening the "Eyes Only" package. Having typed his papers and lectures, she knew enough to suspect that he may have obtained the guide of the sixty-fourth instruction. Then, she read his explanation and viewed the second copper scroll as a way out. She would sell it for millions, divorce her husband, and start over, this time with unlimited resources.

She visualized three barriers to be overcome:

First, to stay safe, she had to find a way to divert attention from her. This would be achieved by passing the "Eyes Only" container to the student reporter who witnessed Wadsworth's house explosion.

Carol would substitute a comparable metal container for the one in the envelope. Given the warnings of the scroll's fragile state and the fact that the contents were written in ancient Hebrew, Carol figured Nancy would refrain from risking direct contact with the scroll. Instead, she would find a way to use its existence in the report she was writing. If she did open the container and found the scroll missing, Carol would simply deny any knowledge of the scroll's whereabouts.

Diverting attention to Nancy likely resulted in the explosion that killed her parents. Carol rationalized that there was no way for her to predict that Nancy would place the scroll in a bank, leaving her home and its occupants vulnerable.

Second, she had to verify that the scroll she kept was the real thing. Maybe it would lead the way to the treasure, maybe not. Despite its brittle condition, she had to find a way to have it examined by a respected expert who would agree that it shared the important characteristics of the historic copper scroll. She would have to be able to trust the expert to treat his work as confidential.

Reviewing Dr. Wadsworth's files, she identified a Dr. Harold Horn as a prime candidate. He agreed that the small portion of the scroll he reviewed did comply with the time and materials of the historic scroll. Carol raised the $5,000 he required by selling all of her better jewelry.

Third, she had to find a Middle East collector

willing and able to buy the scroll. She had a list of reliable experts who might be interested. Most were in Jordan and Israel. However, one name, Howard Epstein, who managed an antiquities museum in New York City, was her number one prospect.

Given the violence perpetrated against her boss, she wanted no part of Middle East espionage. She would contact Epstein in an unconventional manner and see if he might be interested.

Carol searched Google and Linked In for information about Howard Epstein. He was a distinguished looking man of middle age. His short black hair, dark-rimmed glasses, and blue eyes cast a handsome profile. Although associated with many organizations that deal with Middle East antiquities, his museum was completely independent. It was funded by income generated by the estate of a multi-millionaire investor in New York real estate. His hobby was collecting Middle East artifacts. His obsession would go on even after his death.

Epstein was a bachelor who ate alone at Smith & Wollensky's French and steakhouse restaurant most nights. With that information, Carol arranged a two-night sleepover for the kids.

******

It was eight o'clock when she spotted Epstein arriving for his reservation. The maître D greeted his customer as an old friend. As was Epstein's preference, he was seated at a corner table for two in the rear of the restaurant. The fact that it was a light Tuesday night crowd would help to keep their meeting private.

Before he knew what was happening, Carol sat down across from her subject. She looked into his eyes with sympathy.

"I'm so sorry. I know this is your quiet time. But, if you give me just a few minutes, I think you will find our conversation worthwhile."

This was New York City. Men of distinction were used to being the subject of all kinds of phony schemes.

Epstein turned to call the maître D back to his table when Carol said the magic words.

"I have what amounts to the guide of the sixty-fourth instruction."

Epstein turned back to his uninvited guest, looking into her eyes with skepticism.

"Who are you, and what do you want?"

"My name is Carol Stark. I was secretary to Professor Wadsworth from the Princeton Seminary. The day before he was killed, he asked me to hold an envelope for him. Then, when he was murdered, I decided to inspect the contents and do with it what he would have wanted.

"The envelope held a long narrative which he

wrote about how he received a second copper scroll with instructions to the treasure of the second temple. He learned that the previously uncovered scroll was a farce, a scheme to send the Romans and others in circles with no hope of ever uncovering the gold, silver, and valuable antiquities of the temple.

"This second scroll was uncovered recently when a modest earthquake shook the Qumran caves near the Dead Sea. It was recovered by an archeology student who knew how to preserve it and turned it over to his uncle, an antiquities dealer in Jordan. He passed it on to Wadsworth as payment for his bravery defending him from vandals many years before."

A waiter approached the table, and Epstein signaled him away.

Epstein looked into her eyes with skepticism.

"If you have the scroll, and it's as valuable as you say, why do you need me?"

"Professor Wadsworth was my supervisor, a man I respected and trusted. He was tortured and then beheaded when he didn't produce the scroll sought by Middle East terrorists. Then, his house was destroyed in a terrible gas explosion.

"The parents of a university reporter covering the story were murdered when their house was bombed in response to their daughter's research on the new scroll.

"Given these developments, I see a different end to all of this."

"The New York Times speculated that a middle of the night bank robbery likely recovered the scroll. Were you involved in that?" Epstein asked.

"No, of course not. But the package recovered in that action was a plant, holding nothing of value."

Epstein was becoming skeptical.

"Why do I see a request for dollars coming?"

Carol looked around the restaurant, suspecting that she may have stayed too long.

"Here's my proposal:

"First, if you agree to the conditions I am setting, I will turn over the new copper scroll and Wadsworth's narrative to you. A university antiquities expert has examined a brief section of the new scroll and found that it is of the right materials, language, and timeframe. His report is on the flash drive I am placing in front of you."

She put the flash drive on her napkin and moved it in front of Epstein.

"Second, as a matter of security, you will photograph each of the materials included and store the results in several locations around the world.

"Third, you will make the scroll and narrative available under guard to public viewing in your museum. Once the public has the contents of the scroll, there will be no further danger from those who have killed to obtain it.

"Fourth, you will contract to have the contents translated into English, also to be made publicly available.

"Fifth, you will provide one million dollars to Nancy Troll to help compensate for the loss of her parents and another million as a donation to the Princeton Seminary.

"Sixth, and finally, you will provide ten million dollars to a bank account I have opened in the Cayman Islands. Its identification number and the method for deposit are also on the flash drive.

"I know this is a lot to absorb, and you will need to think through much of what I have said. However, it is imperative that you remember that until this information is out in the open, the incentive to steal the scroll and go after the treasure remains."

Epstein wasn't sure how he should react. On the one hand, the woman's story was fantastic and could be full of holes. And yet, if she was legitimate, if he could buy the scroll that points the way to the treasure of the second temple, his museum would become a world attraction.

He looked into her eyes with a new intensity.

"If I have questions or want to discuss how we implement your proposal, how do I contact you?"

Carol responded with no delay.

"You must remember that people dealing with this are being killed. I'm sorry, but if we are going to go ahead, I must know in one week's time. Every day that goes by is another opportunity for the terrorists to strike at me and my family. I'm afraid there can be no room for discussion.

"If you are not interested, send an e-mail to Professor Wadsworth at the Princeton Seminary. Simply say that you will not be able to take part in our next event. I have access to his e-mails.

"If I don't see that e-mail by Tuesday, August 27, I will assume that we have a fundamental agreement and that the funds will be provided by the end of the month.

"Let me suggest that you find a bogus reason to close the museum while you prepare to display the scroll. Once it is on display, the incentive to steal it or kill those who have it in their possession dissolves.

"As soon as I can verify that the cash deposits have been made, I will have the Professor's narrative and the scroll and related materials delivered to the museum via the U.S. mail."

CHAPTER 21
WEDNESDAY, AUGUST 21, 2019
TRENTON, NEW JERSEY

The guilt Nancy felt wouldn't go away until the perpetrators who killed her parents were captured, tried, and put to death or sentenced to life in prison. On the positive side, she believed that the terrorists had obtained the second copper scroll in the bank robbery. Thus, there would be no reason for them to go after anyone else.

She pictured them returning to the Middle East, receiving the adulation of their overseers, and then taking part in an expedition to find a treasure that had been waiting undisturbed since the destruction of the second temple. If successful, their payoff would be in the billions of dollars.

Although she felt regret that the terrorists were able to break into her parent's bank and empty their safety deposit box, it freed her and Josh to finish her series of articles, forward it to the Inquirer, and get the notoriety that might lead the CIA and other international agencies to track the killers down. The best result would be their capture before they were able to find and spend the treasure.

Josh decided to take the next semester off and focus on helping Nancy. He would not leave her alone to fend for herself. If someone was going to challenge her in any way, they would have to face him as well.

When Nancy first prepared to meet the Inquirer's feature editor, her parents were alive, she believed the scroll to be secure in their safety deposit box, and the Philadelphia Inquirer appeared ready to consider publication of her series of articles, with the possibility of their participation in producing a TV special.

Nancy would dedicate the next week or two to bringing the story up to date. Josh would assist with research into the bombing of the Troll residence and the break-in at the bank.

For safety's sake, they would not communicate with the Inquirer until their new draft was finished. Josh went grocery shopping on Monday morning when the crowd was modest. Among the groceries, he picked up the day's Inquirer.

A page one article focused on the strange disappearance of Harold Carr. He was profiled as a Drexel University professor with no suspicious activities in his background. He was a middle-aged man dedicated to his family, students, and golf.

Carr was scheduled to meet with an Inquirer editor and Ms. Troll on the morning when her parents' home was bombed. She fled the meeting never to be seen again while he never showed up. Later that day, it was learned that his car was attacked, pushed into a pond. A search of the waters found his cell phone but no body. Whether he was somehow able to escape and go into hiding or was killed by the perpetrators was unknown.

******

The Middle East terrorists seeking recovery of the scroll were meeting in the conference room of a Washington, DC, embassy. The man at the head of the table was unable to contain the rage that was in his heart.

"You fools! We have supplied all the tools you've requested, and all you can do is continue to embarrass Allah and all who favor our cause.

"Yours was a mission of honor...to deny Israel the treasure intended to rebuild its Hebrew temple. And what do you do? You torture and murder a Presbyterian seminary scholar, blow up the home of an innocent, respected citizen, and rob a bank. And what did you get for all this havoc? You not only got nothing of value, but you also convinced local police forces, the FBI, and the CIA to investigate your actions.

"Now, what do you say for yourselves?"

Three men, the targets of their leader's vilification, sat around the table. Each had a clear cup of Arabic tea. Their operations chief, Aamir Abbas, stood to respond. He was dark-skinned with black eyes, a full black beard, and the physique of a professional wrestler.

"Why would the woman writing the exposé place an empty vessel in a bank safety deposit box? She must have concluded that the second scroll was in that sealed container, as did we. Knowing of its fragile condition and not being an expert in handling such objects, she left it alone until it might be revealed during her presentation.

"We know the scroll was provided to Wadsworth by the antiquities dealer who sought him out in Jordan. But the scroll wasn't present when we searched his residence. Either Wadsworth hid the scroll and passed the container on to another party, or that other party passed the empty container on to the reporter as a way of diverting attention from the scroll's location. If we can identify that third party, we will be able to find and recover the scroll."

The leader, without a better alternative, told his men to go ahead.

"Know this, the more time that passes with the scroll out of our possession, the greater the odds that we will fail to ever recover it."

PART FIVE
HOT POTATO

CHAPTER 22

Harold Carr had had enough. He was a Department Chairman at a first-class U.S. university and wasn't used to being a target of violence. He walked into town and picked up the Pocono Record. A page three story described the blatant bank robbery near Yardley and the safe deposit boxes that appeared to be the target of a daring, middle of the night crime. Carr remembered how Nancy intended to place the scroll in her parent's bank. And so, like Nancy and Josh, he concluded the coast was now clear.

He entered the local Verizon store and bought a new phone that was set up to include all the information from the cellphone lost in the pond. Then, he walked back to the cabin and called home.

It took close to an hour to calm his wife down and assure her that he was okay.

"Sweetheart, this was all about the copper scroll antiquity that caused the explosions in Princeton and then Yardley. After I was attacked, I thought it prudent to disappear. Now that the thieves apparently have what they were after, we should be safe. I'm renting a car and should be home this afternoon."

Driving south out of the Poconos, more than anything, Carr wondered about Nancy. Was she in her parents' house when it exploded? Was the script she developed destroyed? Was there a way to move ahead with their project?

Initially, he was pessimistic about the content and value of her proposed work. Now, he believed it held the potential to help explain the course of history after the destruction of the Second Temple.

When calling Nancy's cellphone yielded nothing but dead air, Carr called his buddy at the Inquirer, Editor-in-Chief Hamels.

"We thought you were dead," Hamels said. "What the hell happened to you?"

"They tried to do me in, but I didn't cooperate.

"Did Nancy survive? Do you have the material we developed?"

"Yes, she survived, and no, she left here with the draft articles. We have no clue as to where she is or if she is still working on the presentation."

"Well, I'm on my way home. Give me a chance

to check in at home and the University, and then we can regroup."

CHAPTER 23

THURSDAY, AUGUST 22, 2019
NEW YORK CITY, NY

Howard Epstein was in shock. For fifteen years, he operated a respectable but modest museum in the heart of New York City. His sponsor, now in his eighties, rarely visited the establishment. While the museum's exhibits attracted many tourists interested in the Middle East and its history, the antiquities on display were not headliners. Now, all that was about to change.

If Carol Stark's story was for real, the Singer Mideast Institute was going to be the hottest ticket in New York City and likely the nation. After his visitor exited the restaurant, Epstein returned to his midtown condo. He had to think through his agenda. He had waited for such an opportunity for many years. Now, if he played his cards right, his status and that of his facility would grow exponentially.

His priority was to go through the flash drive and summarize what was being proposed. Regardless, he would not provide the funds requested until he got a supportive opinion from a recognized expert.

The second priority was to think through how the addition to the museum's collections would alter its appearance. Epstein visualized the center of the building devoted to reproductions of the treasure's most valuable relics, as well as the gold and silver bars included. Then, within that display would be the new scroll with a huge map that followed its directions to the treasure.

After putting meat on the bones of these ideas, he would call his mentor, explain what was happening, and seek advice and the funds to carry it off.

******

It was just after two the next day when Epstein was ready to talk to Mr. Singer. Their relationship had always been both cordial and productive. This would be the real test, he thought. How do you react to a development that would greatly enhance the fundamental status of your museum, cost millions, and yet carry the specter of danger?

Singer's cell phone rang just once before he answered.

"How are you, Howard? One of these days, I've got to leave Palm Beach, return to New York City, and visit the town's best museum."

Epstein got right to the subject matter.

"Andy, I have some incredible news you need to consider.

"Have you been following the violence surrounding the killing of the Princeton Seminary Professor, a guy named Wadsworth?"

There was silence as Singer tried to recall what he had learned.

"This first looked like an accidental gas explosion. Then, the press reported that some Middle East terrorists were involved."

"Right," Epstein responded.

"Well, two days ago, I was approached by Wadsworth's former assistant, Carol Stark. She explained that her boss' killing and that of a family in Yardley were tied to a recently discovered copper scroll. It may provide a map that pinpoints the location of the treasure of the Second Temple, now worth in the billions of dollars."

"This sounds like something for a thriller novel," Singer interrupted.

"I know; it is a fantastic story. But what makes it significant for us is the offer she made to me. She claims to have the scroll and wants us to display it in your museum. Once it is out in the open for all to see, she suggests that the violence will end, and the Israelis and others will form expeditions to find and retrieve the treasure by following information on the scroll."

There was silence as Singer considered Epstein's story.

After what seemed like an eternity to Epstein, Singer reacted.

"So, what is all this going to cost our museum?"

Epstein referred to his notes.

"Stark is demanding payments, some to compensate those who have been injured by the terrorists and the rest to reward her for obtaining the scroll and providing it to us. This will total about twelve million dollars.

"At the same time, we would need to make investments in the museum for renovations, improvements to the building, and acquisitions to accompany the scroll. I visualize copies of some of the more spectacular antiquities and replicas of the gold and silver bars included. I'm estimating the cost of enhancements to the museum at two million dollars.

"Finally, we will have to hire experts to translate the scroll into English and to draw a map that would pinpoint the location of the treasure. There may be some kind of map included with the scroll. However, applying it to today's landmarks will likely require significant expertise and initiative. While all this is going ahead, we would hire a topflight security firm to keep our work under wraps. I'm estimating the cost of these added acquisitions at two million.

"Of course, the demand to enter the museum will grow significantly, allowing us to increase our entrance fee. Also, I have ideas for souvenirs we might have prepared and put up for sale that could raise significant funds.

"What you need to appreciate is the speed with which we must proceed. Once we agree to go ahead, the clock starts ticking. If the terrorists become aware of our plans before the scroll is revealed to the public, we could become the next target of deadly violence."

There was silence as Singer contemplated the situation.

Finally, after two minutes, he responded.

"Okay, let's take one issue at a time.

"The money is not a problem. We've been very conservative in our management of the museum. There are at least three sources I could tap into to meet your budget requests. Certainly, the proposed improvements to the building, the exciting new displays, and the increased traffic are all positive developments.

"But I do have two worrisome concerns.

"First, what if the map turns out to be another farce. These maps have been sought for thousands of years, with few, if any, resulting in the treasure they purport to represent. So, we provide the map to the public, supposedly the route to the treasure. Then, treasure hunters from around the world organize expeditions to follow the directions. In the end, no one finds anything of value. The consensus is that the map is Singer's folly, responsible for millions in expedition expenditures with no payback.

"Second, making the map available to anyone willing to visit the museum may be comparable to ringing the bell for the start of the American gold rush. Every treasure hunter, including the terrorists who have no problem murdering their competition, will enter the museum, retrieve the supposed route to the fortune, and undertake an expedition. The conflict and death that ensues could be extensive, with the price laid at our doorstep."

Epstein responded quickly.

"Andy, you make excellent points, and I think we need to think them through and make accommodations. However, if you want to pursue this, you must keep one truth in mind. The terrorists are still out there looking for the map. If the route to the treasure is not in the public domain, they will be eager to kill for it."

Singer paused, thinking through many possibilities. He was up there in years and not used to forcing his brain through the mental calisthenics that were routine in his younger years. Finally, he opened the discussion of new issues.

"I'm wondering to what extent the map is open to interpretation," Singer said. "I've seen some of these maps, and they site rock formations and other geographic structures from thousands of years ago. Who knows if such clues are still relevant or accurately point the way to the treasure. There may be hundreds of ways to interpret the map, each with corresponding routes.

"Maybe what we need to do first is state clearly that we take no responsibility for the accuracy of the map. And second, rather than tracing a single route to the treasure, perhaps we could lay out a full array of possibilities based on different interpretations and assumptions.

"Howard, give me a day to think all this through. I want to consult with some advisors who have given me sound guidance on controversial issues. I'll get back to you by tomorrow afternoon."

"That's fine, Andy. Just remember that the more time it takes to release the scroll and its information to the public, the greater the chance that we could be the next victims of the terrorists."

CHAPTER 24
YEAR 70 AD
THE JUDEAN DESERT

Panic invaded the procession. With their leader gone, the animals in disarray, and the wind and rain making it impossible to restore order, it appeared that this was an ill-fated initiative that could only end in disaster. The rushing water would claim many more of the animals, while the men entrusted with the treasure could only fight to save their own lives.

Then, the unthinkable happened. Another bolt of lightning struck the cart that held Adam's possessions. When the cart flipped over, the piece of Aaron's rod that was to protect the mission was hurled into the air, landing in the hands of Judah, son of Abram. Suddenly, the fear that was in his heart was transformed into inspiration. He looked out over the scene and spotted an area of green growth below, forming a tunnel surrounded by large boulders.

Despite his advanced years and quiet demeanor, he stood on a large rock and addressed the men in a bold manner.

"Leave your carts and your animals. Follow me to the green area below, where we will find shelter and maintain life. When the storm is finished, we will go back and reclaim the surviving bison and wagons."

He held up the piece of Aaron's rod.

"Those from our past who sacrificed to build the temple will not let us fail."

A new determination possessed the congregation. The men left their carts and slowly followed Judah down the hill to an area protected by thick green growth. They were able to stay in place together, avoiding the torrent of water racing down the gullies. Within the hour, the rains decreased in intensity, eventually slowing to a harmless drizzle.

Once again, Judah addressed the men.

"On the first light of day, we will climb back to the clearing, herd the uninjured bison together, find and repair the remaining carts, consolidate cargo, and continue our holy journey."

Three days later, with the advantage of fair and mild weather, Judah led the caravan down the mountain towards their destination.

CHAPTER 25

MONDAY, AUGUST 26, 2019
PRINCETON, NJ

Carol checked Professor Wadsworth's email, finding no message from Epstein. So far, so good. The Director of New York's Singer Mideast Institute was taking her proposal seriously.

Soon, her two children, Larry at ten and Jamie at twelve, would be back in school. Friday was their last day at the community center day camp. They had spent the summer between traditional camp sports and field trips to a variety of sites in the area. Their last trip, scheduled for today, would be to the beach at Asbury Park.

Once the kids were back in school, she would focus on her marriage, i.e., the end of her ties to Roger Stark. She had already consulted with an attorney. He counseled that her husband's gambling problem and huge debt would form an adequate justification for divorce. The fact that she would not be interested in receiving any compensation from him would streamline the proceedings.

It was a hot summer's day. She would celebrate the success of her plans by spending most of the day at their neighborhood pool. Then, she would go to the store and purchase groceries for a backyard cookout with the kids. The camp bus was scheduled to arrive at four-thirty.

It was ten minutes after five, and Carol was beginning to worry. After a field trip, it wasn't unusual for the kids to arrive somewhat late. But, for the first time, she was beginning to wonder if those seeking the treasure might be on to her.

She could have tried to isolate the children by sending them to her parents' home in Wisconsin. But her guiding principle was to keep everything the same. Not to betray the scheme that would make her a very wealthy woman.

Before she would consider the painful alternatives, she decided to call the camp office and check on the bus. Maybe it was simply running late. She walked into the kitchen, sat at the kitchen table, and dialed her cellphone. The camp administrator picked up right away.

"Hello, Community Center Day Camp."

"Is that you, Carl?" she asked.

"Hi Carol, what can we do for you?"

"Is the bus running late today? It hasn't arrived at our house yet."

There was a delay as the Administrator checked to see if any other late complaints had been received.

"Nope, looks like we're running on time.

"But Carol, did you forget? You sent a text that your husband would pick the kids up at the Center before the bus left on its afternoon run. Something about you all going out for dinner tonight."

It was a dagger in her heart. Somehow, the devils who killed her boss and blew up the home of an innocent family had turned their attention to her; specifically, to her two children.

She ended the call with the Administrator, blaming it on forgetfulness due to her husband's absence on a business trip. Then, she hung up and contemplated the consequences.

Were the kids being tortured? Would she receive a finger or ear in the mail, indicating that nothing was beyond their depravity until they received the scroll? If she gave them the scroll, would they return the kids, or would she never see them again?

Should she call the police or FBI, those investigating the murder of her boss and the explosion of the house in Yardley? If she sought help from the authorities, would she have to admit to the get rich scheme she devised?

In any case, she would not contact Epstein or let him know that something was wrong. If the kidnappers required the scroll before they would free the kids, the game was up. In that case, she couldn't provide the museum with their breakthrough display, and they would have no reason to turn over the funds.

******

This was the first Zoom meeting of the authorities investigating the two house explosions, the murder of Professor Wadsworth, the mysterious bank robbery, and the missing principals. It was 4:00 pm, and the group was anxious to get started. Most had been working around the clock to find the guilty parties and take them out of the public domain.

FBI Regional Chief Joan MacLennan led the discussion:

"Our work, with the assistance of the CIA, has led us to the Iranian Embassy in Washington. An unnamed source tells us that the Iranians became aware of the newly discovered copper scroll after it was smuggled from caves near the Dead Sea to an antiquities dealer in Jordan. They lost track of it before it was provided to Wadsworth as payment for his bravery many years before.

"Wadsworth's murder was carried out by a team assembled by the Iranians. Their goal is to deny the

Israelis the billions of dollars in gold, silver, and temple antiquities associated with the map provided by the scroll. They would accomplish this by discovering the route to the treasure first, retrieving its valuables, and providing them to the Iranian government in Tehran. They assume that unless they can capture the scroll and keep it from the Israelis, the Jewish state will find a way to follow it and assume ownership over what was originally theirs.

"We are analyzing several photos provided through security cameras in active locations. Once we have adequate evidence, we'll pick up the offenders and bring them into custody. If they are Iranian, we will try to prosecute them or, at the very least, expel them from the U.S. and issue sanctions against the Iranian government."

Commander Auburn raised several related issues.

"We are making some progress in tracking the locations of the student reporter, Nancy Troll from Drexel, and Josh Rosenberg, a student at Stockton working down the shore. Apparently, the two met one night at a bar in Margate and have been a hot item ever since.

"With her parents murdered in the house explosion, we believe the two have found a hideaway where they are still working on the feature articles promised to the Inquirer. A comprehensive search of locations associated with their friends and relatives should yield results soon."

Alvin Harrison, the Pennsylvania representative, picked up the ball.

"We continue to pursue leads to the house explosion and bank robbery. However, I'd like to raise what I think is an important question. Have the Iranians or another party or parties actually located the scroll?

"If the scroll is in the possession of one of the offenders, I would assume that the violence will cease as they leave the country and attempt to use the map to find and cash in the treasure. If it is still being kept by a Wadsworth disciple, i.e., Troll or Rosenberg, or another party, then I think we can expect the violence to continue.

"In another matter, we are continuing to look for Harold Carr, the Drexel advisor to Troll. We know there was an attempt on his life, but we aren't convinced that it was successful. He is a respected administrator at Drexel, and we will continue to search for him."

MacLennan summarized their status and set the direction for the near future.

"Thanks. I believe we are on the right track. If the violence ends, and the culprits have recovered the scroll, the emphasis shifts to the Middle East as they try to uncover the treasure. That responsibility will rest with the CIA.

"However, we will continue to seek and prosecute those responsible for the crimes already committed. If they are still looking for the scroll, and there is more violence, we continue our current course. Hopefully, we will be able to find those responsible and head them off before there are more victims.

"Let's bring this session to a close and meet tomorrow at 4:00 pm."

CHAPTER 26

TUESDAY, AUGUST 27, 2019

PRINCETON, NJ

It was seven o'clock, and Carol was in a state of panic. She was trapped by her own ingenuity. Her efforts to trade a foreign treasure for millions and realize independence from her husband had put the lives of her children, her most precious, in deadly jeopardy. She needed to ensure the safety of her children while continuing her plan to obtain incredible wealth and security.

She concluded that the only way out was to convince the kidnappers that she had no knowledge of the scroll and would not be able to help them even if she wanted to. Despite her drive to leave her husband, as a first step, she called him. She never doubted their love for one another. The problem wasn't emotional but his inability to leave a gambling habit that had taken over his life.

Carol explained to Robert that the kids going missing may have been the result of her close relationship with Professor Wadsworth. The men seeking the scroll may have concluded that she somehow received the scroll and could be coerced into turning it over to them. Kidnapping her children may have been their way to capture the scroll.

He told her to sit tight. He would be home in a couple of hours, and they would deal with the situation together.

Beginning to cry, she said they should contact the police immediately. He convinced her to wait, claiming that there may be more than one way to handle this and keep the kids safe.

******

Robert Stark sat behind the wheel of his new Mercedes. He would keep his speed at the legal limit, making sure he would not be interrupted. The trip from Atlantic City to Princeton would take no more than two hours.

The kids going missing was his worst nightmare. With his gambling debt now in six figures, he violated one of his crucial rules, dealing with underworld figures who would threaten life and limb.

He was a super salesperson, helping to increase the profits of Labtech to record levels. This is a firm that provides chemicals and expertise to allow exact analyses of a huge variety of laboratory tests. Traveling throughout the East Coast, his job was a perfect setup for a man being consumed by the thrill of gambling on sports.

He traveled from town to town, during the day contacting a list of potential buyers. Overnight, he would scour the Internet for opportunities to parlay his knowledge into winning bets. He truly believed that he was superior to the oddsmakers establishing the competition.

When his latest round of wagers fell well short of expectations, he sought and found a sponsor who advanced him one hundred thousand dollars. He used half to forestall the threats of loan sharks in three locations and bet a five-game football parlay with the rest. When the parlay wager came up one game short, his house of cards crashed to the ground. Unable to borrow any more funds, he didn't know where to turn.

Then, he received the call from Carol. The kids were gone with no explanation.

Someone planted the story that they would not be on the camp bus because they were all going out to dinner. While Carol reasoned that the kids were being held by sources involved with the copper scroll, Robert saw those to whom he owed his gambling debt as the more likely culprits.

Robert pulled his new vehicle into the driveway. Carol was waiting on the front porch. After a cold embrace, they sat at the backyard deck's umbrella table, each regretting the steps they had taken. The anger each felt was consumed by worry over their children's wellbeing. Robert initiated their life and death conversation.

"Before we decide on our best course of action, we need to fully discuss what got us here. What was the deal with Wadsworth and how might you figure in it?"

Carol responded with mixed emotions. On the one hand, it was comforting to have a partner again, someone to help think through the best course of action. On the other hand, now she was working with the man who precipitated the danger she and the kids were in.

Regardless, she went on to explain the entire affair. How Wadsworth was killed by Middle East sources seeking a copper scroll that promised to identify the location of billions in gold, silver, and religious antiquities; how she came into the possession of the scroll and schemed to make it appear that she had passed it on to an ambitious reporter; how the reporter's home was destroyed by an explosion; and how a package that she prepared, absent the scroll, was stolen from a local bank.

Listening to this fantastic chronology, Robert sat in amazement, previously unaware of the adventuresome side of his own wife.

"So, do you have the real scroll?"

"Well, yes, and no. Yes, I have it. But the longer it is in my possession, the greater the danger that Middle East sources will take it away using the kind of violence on which they rely. And so, I've cut a deal with a New York City Museum to provide it to them for a price. Once the scroll and its map are out in the open, it will be too late for those seeking it with terror and brutality."

"What kind of price?" Robert asked.

"Ten million to be deposited to an account I've established in the Caymans."

"And have you received any kind of a ransom note proposing a trade, the kids for the scroll?"

"Not a word," she replied. "That's why I waited to speak with you before calling the police. Given your betting record, I'm wondering if you've gotten in over your head again, and the kids are being used to get you to pay up."

Robert got up, walked into the house, and poured two of their favorite drinks, Canadian Mist and Vodka. Then, he returned to the deck, offering one of the drinks to Carol.

"I'm so sorry. I had to borrow some real money to pay off several smaller wagers. The source of the big money has been known to apply physical restraints.

Driving home, I received an email from them saying that they would return the kids uninjured when the loan is paid plus a twenty-five-thousand-dollar penalty."

"So, what do you need to get in the clear?" Carol asked.

"Two hundred and twenty-five thousand dollars," Robert responded.

"I know you've heard it before, but if we can pay it all off and get the kids out of this, it will be the end of my gambling. I can't be responsible for the deaths of innocent children who we love and who love us."

Carol had heard it before. For some reason, this time, she believed the man who swept her off her feet ten years before and gave her two wonderful children. When his debts were paid in full, and Robert once again was able to focus on her, the kids, and his job, they would be free to live the ideal life promised by the Princeton community.

PART SIX
MOVING THE MONEY

CHAPTER 27
WEDNESDAY AUGUST 28, 2019
TRENTON, NJ

Josh and Nancy were working around the clock. Much of the written word had already been put to bed. The task now was to update the status of the players and try to assign blame for the deaths that had occurred. Once complete, they would drive to the Inquirer's office and provide the package to the Editor. They would not call in advance, fearing discovery by those dedicated to obtaining the scroll and its map.

Since their retreat to the Trenton property, every day at noon, Nancy replaced the battery in her cellphone, trying to call her mentor, Professor Carr. Until today, there was no response. But today, for the first time since their escape, his phone rang. Her heartbeat accelerated, and Nancy's breathing became labored. Then, a familiar voice answered the phone.

"Is that you, Nancy? Are you okay?"

She took a deep breath and tried to respond. When no words left her mouth, she feared that he would hang up.

Finally, she was able to communicate.

"Professor, yes, it's Nancy. We've tried to call you every day, but there was no response. What happened to you?"

"The morning we were to meet with the Inquirer, they went after me with a drone, knocked my car into a pond, and left me for dead. I was able to flee the scene and make my way to a cottage in the Poconos. Once I heard of the break-in at the Yardley bank, I assumed that they got what they were after, and the coast is now clear. But, of course, there is no guarantee of that.

"What's your status?" Professor Carr asked.

"I was waiting for you at the Inquirer when they blew up my house and killed my parents. The Editor wanted me to wait for the authorities, but I had to get out and think it through on my own. I kept calling you to see if you were okay but never got an answer. Then, I called Josh, my boyfriend, and we both fled to a secure location. We've been here ever since, working on the story.

"Your adventure, Professor, could add another exciting chapter to the story."

"I'll write a factual account of what happened and send it to you via email. Then, you can work it into the story.

"I'm so sorry about your parents. Dealing in the news has become more dangerous than ever. I hope you don't blame yourself. You were only seeking the truth.

"And don't feel like you need to answer every question. In fact, at the end of your presentation, you should list the important unknowns: who killed Wadsworth and why; were the same parties responsible for the deaths of your parents; how does the bank robbery fit into all this; is an ancient copper scroll behind it all?

"What's your target date for delivering the story to the Inquirer?"

"Once we receive the description of your latest adventure, we'll be ready in one or two days. Then, let's try again to meet with the Editor and discuss the text and, hopefully, a TV special."

"I'll call the Editor and alert him to our timeline. If all goes as expected, let's target Tuesday, September 3, to meet with the Inquirer.

CHAPTER 28

Almost two weeks had passed since Carol introduced her proposal to Howard Epstein. Despite the need for a speedy resolution of the related issues, Andy Singer, Epstein's sponsor insisted that each issue be thoroughly explored with follow-up steps taken as soon as possible.

Two days after Epstein relayed his proposal, Singer chartered a private jet from Palm Springs to La Guardia. After a night's rest at his condo in Midtown West, he was ready to meet with Epstein to move things along. They met at 10:00 am in Singer's second-floor office at the museum, which, according to posted notices, was closed to meet updated city safety requirements.

After opening niceties, Singer got down to business.

"Have you received any complaints about the closure?"

"I had to notify two summer camp groups scheduled to be here today and tomorrow. I've refunded their payments and offered free tours in the fall. I've also given the staff a few days off while we chart our course. When they see what's coming, they'll be ecstatic."

"If all the open questions can be effectively answered, I've freed up the dollars to compensate those identified and to initiate the museum's renovation."

Epstein shifted in his chair, anxious to move the changes forward.

"That's great, Andy."

"From what my lawyers tell me, the key is to portray the material displayed as antiquities whose accuracy is open to question until expeditions verify their claims.

"What are the results from your efforts to verify the legitimacy of the scroll and the guide provided?" Singer asked.

"In addition to the positive findings of their expert, a Harold Horn, PhD, we were given two samples to examine: first, a couple of pages from the copper scroll, which is written in ancient Hebrew; and second, the beginnings of a map to the treasures of the second Temple. Based upon the conclusions of our experts on staff, the materials, language, and their age are all legitimate."

"Okay, then, we need to transfer the funds promised. At the same time, I want to quietly initiate discussions with the architects who we might use to transform the museum. As soon as we have the entire package, we need to display it and get the word out to a wide audience."

Epstein injected a word of caution.

"As we open the display, we need to inform those interested that these new materials have been thoroughly videoed and duplicated and are being stored in several locations. Stealing the displays or destroying them will not provide criminal elements with an advantage."

"In that regard, Howard, let's spend the next day or two putting together a list of tasks and their priorities. Then, as soon as the materials arrive, we need to race to video them and place them on display."

"I'll see if our architects might supply preliminary stations to accommodate immediate displays. Then, after they have time to provide models of the final designs, we can review their ideas and determine the changes and additions to be made to the museum.

"And while this work is going ahead, let's employ a security firm to make sure we are left alone.

The last thing we need is Middle East thugs intervening with our work, trying to steal the scroll and map before we have a chance to copy and release them."

******

Dr. Harold Horn sat in a first-class seat on a flight from Kennedy Airport to Saint Martin. He scored an unexpected windfall and wasn't sticking around to give others an opportunity to question him.

He was asked to evaluate the legitimacy of a copper scroll and related materials. His extensive experience assessing antiquities, studying the history of their development, and lecturing at respected universities made him an excellent choice for such tasks.

Interrupting work on an upcoming book on which he had been focusing for over a year, he demanded and received five thousand dollars for what amounted to two days' work. Then, out of the blue, an association of Middle East researchers asked him to fill out a survey form concerning the subjects of recent work assignments. One of the questions concerned a copper scroll. Once again, the fee was five thousand dollars.

Recently divorced, with no children, he decided to take a week off and enjoy the clear blue waters and French cooking of his favorite Saint Martin resort.

The survey, secretly designed by the Iranians

seeking the scroll and its related components, was specifically intended to collect information from those who might be evaluating the corresponding materials. Three experts provided feedback that could be indicative of the right items. However, Horn's information, especially concerning a copper scroll, was the best fit.

Within six hours, a blanket of electronic and human surveillance surrounded the New York museum for whom Horn consulted. They would head off all incoming packages that might conform to the treasure's content. The fact that the museum recently closed for renovations added to the suspicion that this was the location that would be receiving the prize.

******

Surprisingly, another party read much into the survey. With Nancy writing their report full-time, Josh was free to explore related information. His Google search for information on a second copper scroll was a long shot. But it uncovered the survey. He was unable to track down the survey's sponsor. However, speculation with Nancy was enlightening.

"So, who would be interested in staff researching a second copper scroll?"

"Maybe we have been looking at this all wrong. What if someone has the scroll and is looking to have it blessed by experts? That step would be required before any sale takes place."

"Assume that the package stolen from the bank failed to provide the scroll and its related materials," she concluded. "What if the source seeking the scroll at any cost is getting ready to pay for it and wants information to verify its authenticity?"

"We need to include that possibility in our report."

******

FBI Chief Joan MacLennan was walking back to her office after updating her superiors on the investigation of the copper scroll mystery. A communications staffer rushed down the hall after her.

"Chief MacLennan, I may have some important information for you. Can we meet?"

"Of course," she said. "Let's sit in my office."

They turned the corner, and she opened the door to her suite of rooms. She walked into her personal station and invited the staffer to sit.

"So, what's going on?"

"Since we received the CIA report that the Iranians are likely responsible for the murders associated with the copper scroll, we have launched an initiative to see if there are any unusual efforts on their part to seek information on relevant antiquities. It looks like they have placed a communications blanket around certain locations in New York City, specifically, the Antiquities Museum operated by the Singer Group. If that museum has planned to purchase the scroll, I assume the Iranians are working to intervene and grab the prize before any transfer takes place."

"Well, if the Iranians don't have the scroll, who the hell does?"

"We detected communications between the museum's manager, Howard Epstein, and a lady named Carol Stark. She was the assistant to Professor Wadsworth before he was killed."

"So, what are you concluding? That Stark has had the scroll all along and is trying to sell it to the Iranians?"

"Yes and no. It makes sense to conclude that she has had the scroll from the beginning. However, my guess is that she is attempting to sell it to the museum. The Iranians will try to take the scroll away before the museum can take possession."

"So, if we can use the scroll as bait, we should be able to catch the Iranians in the act. Then, we can prosecute them for the murders, or at least expel them from the U.S. and sanction the Iranian government."

"Make sure that we don't block any money transfers attempted by the museum. According to Legal, it's difficult, if not impossible, to assign ownership of antiquities. It all depends on how far back you want to go.

"The fact that the museum will share the content of the scroll with the public should end the domestic violence we've witnessed."

CHAPTER 29
YEAR 70 AD
THE JUDEAN DESERT

Judah led the procession of carts down the Judean desert with skill and understanding. He was a leader of necessity. He displayed enthusiasm as they made progress towards the Dead Sea. With the weather clearing, he had one serious problem. He wasn't sure where they were supposed to be going.

Adam Levi had scouted the area before their journey began. He located a safe place to camp in the mountains bordering the Dead Sea. Once he organized the men who agreed to guard their position and secure the treasure under the ground, they would descend to the area bordering the Sea and deposit the Temple valuables.

But Judah wasn't privy to any of the discussions that reviewed and then finalized Levi's plan. Unless those who agreed to help contacted him, he would be on his own. He would have to find his way to a proper location, devise a scheme to deposit the Temple antiquities, gold, and silver, and record the position for others who would retrieve the valuables when the coast cleared.

"We will rely upon the Lord to show us the way," he proclaimed.

The caravan deliberately made its way down green hills and valleys. The oxen were obviously spent but Judah figured they would last one more day, all that they would need to approach the sea. Finally, as the sun was setting on the sixth day of their journey, the men in the lead cart cheered. They were able to see the white sands and aqua blue waters of the Dead Sea.

Judah recruited six volunteers to scout the shoreline for the fissure Levi had located. As night fell, the group pitched their tents and secured and fed the animals. Having survived the worst of conditions, pride and confidence spread among them.

A full moon rose, casting a bright light on their surroundings. One of the scouts spotted a great fissure not too far from the campsite. Whether the crater was Levi's resting place for the treasure or not, no one knew. But the dimensions and the lining of thick tar fit the description. Sunrise would signal the expedition to prepare the treasure for its deposit by the Great Salt Sea.

CHAPTER 30
SATURDAY AUGUST 31, 2019
NEW YORK CITY, NY

On Saturday morning, The Singer Group's electronic transfers of funds took effect: one million dollars to Nancy Troll, one million to the Princeton Seminary, and ten million to Carol Stark in her newly established Cayman account. Carol had assured Epstein that when she was notified of the funding transfers, the package containing the scroll would be on its way through the U.S. Mail.

Wadsworth's narrative, the second copper scroll, including a map that tracked the treasure's location from Jerusalem to a site near the Dead Sea, were ready to go. Carol had placed the materials in a secure carton protected by state-of-the-art insulation. The package would display U.S. Postal one-day delivery service, including tracking information.

All she had to do was drop the carton at her

local post office and pay the modest fee. When she received notice that the delivery had been made and the receiving party signed for it, her Middle East adventure would be over.

At the same time, Robert would initiate a wire transfer to the gamblers holding the kids. According to Robert, the deep pockets reflected in that payment would ensure compliance by the men holding the children. If he could afford the ransom, they would have no doubt it wouldn't be long before Robert was back on the Internet, risking more.

It was eleven in the morning. Carol and Robert sat at the kitchen table, waiting for notification that the funds from the Museum had been received.

"It's hard for me to believe that you engineered such a complex and opulent deal. I've always known how smart you are but never dreamed you would use your capabilities in such a way."

Carol looked into Robert's eyes.

"Sometimes you just do what you must do. When the copper scroll fell into my lap, I couldn't deny the opportunity, especially given the money troubles created by your gambling."

"Well, if this comes off, we should be able to enjoy ourselves for many years to come, thanks to you and Professor Wadsworth," Robert responded.

******

Howard Epstein and Andy Singer sat in Singer's second-floor museum office. Orders for the funds transfers had been given to Chase's Singer representative, Orin Reed. An email confirmed that the three transactions were initiated by 11:00 am.

Carol had been assured by her Cayman banking contact that she would be informed of anticipated deposits within a half hour of their occurrence. It was ten past noon, and she and Robert were approaching panic. If the promised deposit was not made, their children's lives would be in jeopardy. At the same time, no deposit meant no delivery of the copper scroll. The longer it was in her possession, the greater the danger that those who have killed for it would come calling.

Then, a secure email from their Cayman bank verified that the ten-million-dollar deposit had been made.

"Okay," Carol said. "As we agreed, I'll deliver the goods to the post office, and you pay off your gambling debt."

Driving the twelve blocks to the local post office was filled with worry. This was the ultimate test of Carol's belief that using routine processes would protect the recognition of her treasure transactions.

The other concern was more personal. She was trusting the man whose weakness resulted in the kidnapping. What if he paid off the debt, made arrangements for the kid's return, and then took off with the remaining funds, most of the ten million dollars? Was his love for her and the kids enough to ignore the gambling opportunities provided by the funds she received for her ingenuity?

She pulled into the parking lot of the post office as she had done many times before. Then, she exited the car, obtained the package from the rear section of the SUV, and carried it into the modest building. There were two ahead of her in line. When her turn came, she put the neatly wrapped carton on the counter, just ahead of the 1:00 pm closing time.

"Did you want the insurance?" asked an African American lady behind the counter.

"No," Carol answered. "Just a few old books we're donating. But we promised to get them there quickly for a display."

"Since Monday is Labor Day, your package will be delivered on Tuesday morning, September 3."

"That's fine," Carol responded.

The woman weighed the package, generated the stamps, pasted them on, and created a bill for $27.50.

Carol placed her VISA card in the receptor, signed for it, and removed her card and the receipt.

"Thank you," Carol said as the clerk picked up the carton and placed it in a pile of packages scheduled to be delivered on Tuesday.

Back in the car, Carol dialed Epstein.

"Hello, Singer Antiquities Museum. This is Howard Epstein."

"Howard, this is Carol. Since Monday is Labor Day, your package is due for delivery by U.S. Mail on Tuesday morning. Best of luck."

Then, she ended the call, her responsibilities completed.

******

Back at the house, Robert was struggling with his assignment. He had the email address of the kidnappers. However, he wasn't sure how he should proceed, transferring the two-hundred and twenty-five thousand dollars while making sure that the kids would be released.

Eventually, he asked his contact to call so they could discuss the details. Within minutes, the phone rang, and he picked up.

"Hello."

"Let's make this quick and clean. I'll give you my account and you send the total owed. Within minutes, I'll send the order to release the kids and have them returned. And by the way, they are unaware that they have been held against your will. They think you paid for a vacation trip at the conclusion of summer."

"Okay then. You'll get your money within the hour. And how will the kids be transported home?"

"They'll be dropped off tomorrow afternoon at the Community Center. Note that the staff supervising them also has no hint that the kids were part of an involuntary transaction.

"And, by the way, next time you are in the mood to bet a lot of money, make sure you have the backing to pay off in case your hunches don't come true."

With that, the line went dead. If the kid's lives were not at stake, Robert was tempted to screw the deal and walk away with ten million dollars. But he couldn't live with himself or Carol if the transaction didn't work out. He turned to the instructions left by his partner and transferred the funds.

CHAPTER 31
SUNDAY SEPTEMBER 1, 2019

Carol and Robert hadn't slept together in months. His growing debt, her get rich scheme, and the dangers posed by Middle East sources put their physical liaisons on the back burner. The threat to their two children, in the hands of professional gamblers, overshadowed all the rest.

But now, their world appeared to be refreshed, offering a new life and love. Her manipulation of the second copper scroll provided the wealth that was on the way to putting Robert in the clear with his gambling debt, enabling the return of their children, and offering a carefree Princeton lifestyle. In recognition of their renaissance, they slept together for the first time in a long time, reviving the physical contact that fulfilled their dreams.

******

Since Professor Wadsworth's gruesome murder,

Director Parnes was living in a difficult environment. Thinking back, he searched for steps he might have taken to avoid the loss of his best instructor and researcher. If he had advised Wadsworth to immediately turn over the scroll to the Israelis, likely the original owners, he might still be alive. But, by the time he was aware of the package sent by Wadsworth's Jordanian associate, it was already too late.

Parnes sought to erase the grim picture of deadly violence played out in Wadsworth's home, just a few blocks from the Seminary's campus. When he learned of a one-million-dollar donation provided anonymously, he made plans to use it to establish a research chair in Wadsworth's name and to construct a statue honoring his contributions to the Seminary.

******

Nancy, Josh, and Professor Carr were ready to meet with the Inquirer. Their series of articles, including Carr's harrowing experience, was complete. While the current status of the copper scroll and its related materials was still unknown, based on Josh's research, their likely sale appeared to be imminent.

Given the danger posed by those seeking the scroll, Editor-In-Chief Ralph Hamel suggested that they meet on Sunday, along with three Assistant Editors. Nancy provided oral summaries of each of the three proposed articles. Josh described the visual aids they were suggesting. Carr offered historical perspectives from the newly discovered scroll.

Hamel invited a representative of Philadelphia's TV Chanel Six, to sit in. He invited the three to take part in an hour-long interview that would cover the highlights of the three articles.

Nancy was flabbergasted by the one-million-dollar anonymous deposit made to her savings account. She had lost much: the parents she loved and the home she grew up in. The money wouldn't bring them back but would allow her the freedom to finish her studies and explore promising career opportunities.

Despite, or maybe because of their adventuresome history, Nancy and Josh continued their loving relationship. They were a unit that would face the future together.

******

The Iranians were ready to move, once again, to retrieve the copper scroll.

When they learned that the Singer Antiquities Museum had purchased the scroll, they entrusted a Special Forces Group to design an action plan to intervene and retrieve the prize. Of course, this was New York City, not some rural area in the Middle East. They had to adjust their methods to apply to an urban area with dense automobile traffic and significant numbers of shoppers. Based upon the hacking of the Museum's telephone conversations, they were flabbergasted to learn that the scroll was being delivered on Tuesday morning by U.S. Mail.

Their strategy was to focus on the U.S. Postal Service mail truck and the driver who would make the proper stop, identify the packages addressed to the museum, load them onto a dolly transport cart, and move them to the building area where cartons were received.

A large drone parked above the Singer Antiquities Museum would ensure their final success. If anyone interfered with their efforts to intercept the scroll, they would be shot down from above. A smaller drone, designed to transport packages, was waiting in a delivery truck parked outside the museum.

When the mail truck parked, the delivery drone would be removed from its truck and set up in the street. The men dealing with the drone would wear New York City Policeman uniforms.

When the mail carrier loaded the packages onto the dolly, the Iranians would strike. They would shoot the driver with a tranquilizer gun and load the packages onto the smaller drone. Then, the drone would take off and fly the scroll and accompanying material out of the area and eventually to a jet transport that would fly to the Iranian capital.

The men involved would leave the scene in the

delivery truck and be transported to the safety of the Iranian Embassy on Third Avenue.

With their mission completed, the large drone would abandon the area, landing at a private jetport in New Jersey.

CHAPTER 32
YEAR 70 AD
THE GREAT SALT SEA

The sun rose on another beautiful day by the Great Salt Sea. Daylight seemed to confirm the suitable nature of the site found the night before.

Judah organized the men into three teams. The first team would examine the site again, remove any debris found, and find the best burial area within the tar fissure. The second team would use the oxen to transport the gold and silver to the edge of the fissure. And the third team would inspect the temple antiquities, rewrap those requiring attention, and transport them to the site.

Judah addressed his men:

"We must complete our work with abandon. Should a Roman legion become aware of the valuables we are depositing all will be lost. Our goal is to transport all materials to the site and then into the fissure later today. Tomorrow, we will overlay the deposits with the wood cover prepared to protect and disguise our riches. Finally, we must place a thin layer of tar and surrounding soil over the wood."

While the men worked, Judah verified the inventory prepared before the start of their journey. There were some losses when the storm took some of the carts, but most of the valuables were preserved.

Then, he turned his attention to preparing a map that would lead a future generation to the treasures of the Second Temple. He began from the location of the tar pit and worked his way back to the Temple. All along the route, he noted landmarks that were sure to be sustained over time.

When they arrived, Judah met with Emanuel Hakkov, the Temple treasurer, the Temple High Priest, and others from temple leadership. Judah provided his report:

"Although we lost our leader, Adam Levi, and several brave souls during a mighty storm, our journey to preserve the Temple treasures has been completed. Tomorrow, I will provide a map that will document the route to our treasures for future generations. I suggest that it be preserved as a copper scroll.

"I am returning the piece of Aaron's Rod which gave me the strength to lead this momentous endeavor. I hope you will provide it to another soul seeking justice in the name of our Lord."

CHAPTER 33
TUESDAY, SEPTEMBER 3, 2019

The Singer Antiquities Museum is a three-story structure of amber-colored brick. A central section allows visitors to enter up twelve steps and then into a large lobby. More than a dozen windows face the street not far from Lincoln Square. Thick green ivy randomly accents the colorful presentation.

A basement entrance, down seven steps, at the right corner of the building is the package drop-off. A buzzer allows delivery staff to notify museum personnel of pending deliveries. Three beeps signal the need for staff sign-off.

It was a warm, sunny day with most residents, office staff, and shoppers seeking the cool of indoor air-conditioned locations. The Iranians took comfort in the light traffic and very few pedestrians in the area. They had yet to see a policeman. It was 11:25am, and there was no sign of the mail truck.

Then, a standard U.S. Mail truck appeared. Driving slowly down the street, it double-parked in front of the museum. This set the Iranian plan into motion.

The delivery drone was removed from a truck parked in front of the grey office building next to the museum. Three men were required to rig the drone for flight.

Just as the drone was ready to accept the treasure, a mail carrier exited his truck and opened the rear baggage compartment. He removed four cartons, placing them on a dolly transport. As he began moving towards the museum's delivery entry point, one of the men who worked on setting up the drone fired a dart into the mailman's chest. The mail carrier hit the ground hard while his dolly moved on its own to the edge of the sidewalk.

With the drone ready, two members of their team removed the four cartons on the dolly and secured them within a drone compartment. One of the men manipulated the controls that initiated propeller action. Within seconds, the drone took off. They watched as the treasure made its way into the sky.

With no hint of opposition, the large overhead drone moved slowly away while the ground team entered their truck. It pulled away from the curb and headed unincumbered to the Iranian embassy.

******

The inside of the museum was an armed camp.

On Sunday, FBI Chief Joan MacLennan decided to spring into action. She visited the post office site from which Carol was sending the scroll. Clearing her action with the Postmaster General, she removed Carol's package, substituting a very similar carton.

It was early the next evening when Harold Epstein, always a creature of habit, sat at his usual table at Smith & Wollensky. A beautiful woman, smartly dressed, approached. Remembering Carol's introduction, Epstein rose to face her. They hugged, and MacLennan whispered in his ear.

"FBI, please go along."

They shared a fine dinner and a bottle of wine. Before dessert, Joan suggested that Howard order some carry-out food for the staff in the museum.

After he paid the check, a waiter provided him with a large carry-out bag. Epstein and MacLennan hugged again and said farewell. Then, Joan left to spend the night with a girlfriend and Epstein returned to the Museum, grasping the bag that contained the scroll and its related materials.

The imitation package provided by the FBI and stolen by the Iranians wasn't opened until it was flown to the Iranian capital. Once again, their attempt to possess the scroll and retrieve the treasure met with frustration. When the men behind much of the violence left the Iranian Embassy, they were arrested and held on serious federal charges.

******

One week after the scroll was provided to Epstein, the museum was ready with an advance display of the scroll and map, supposedly leading antiquities treasure hunters to their objective. One section of the display explained how foreign interests murdered Professor Wadsworth, killed the parents of a young student reporter, attacked a university professor, and blew up a bank, all in the name of retrieving the scroll.

With articles published by the Philadelphia Inquirer, ABC TV coverage, and features offered by other newspapers and cable news stations, much of the public became fascinated by the copper scroll and its promise. The Singer Antiquities Museum became New York's hottest tourist ticket, with lines around the block a common occurrence.

Soon, it was rumored that the Israeli antiquities officials had launched an initiative to follow the scroll to the treasure of the Second Temple.

EPILOGUE

Although the main characters in this adventure suffered serious losses, some also benefitted in unpredictable ways.

Nancy and Josh finished their studies, married, and took an apartment in Philadelphia. Nancy works full-time as a reporter with the Philadelphia Inquirer. Her focus is on covering complex stories that are not easy to explain and may have hidden consequences for the public. Josh is employed by a local architecture firm. He lends his support to Nancy when construction or established buildings figure in her research.

With the millions they received from the Singer Antiquities Museum, Carol and Robert were able to turn their lives around. With no debts hanging over his head and his sports betting a thing of the past, Robert established a small consulting firm that specialized in data analysis. Carol, in addition to caring for the kids, organized efforts to obtain charitable contributions for the Princeton Seminary.

Joan MacLennan continued to move up in the ranks of FBI intelligence. Her personal involvement in defeating the Iranian attempt to capture the copper scroll and arresting those involved in terrorist activity was recognized by her receipt of the FBI Medal for Meritorious Achievement.

Andy Singer and Howard Epstein continue to enjoy the glow radiated by their revamped facility, including the display of the copper scroll. While the Israelis never announced that they were able to follow the scroll to the treasure, several antiquities from that period had been donated to the museum by the Israeli government. The risk Singer took in providing the funds requested paid off for his facility and may have provided huge benefits for the Israelis.

Professor Carr's survival in the face of the Iranian drone attack and submersion in a local pond caused him to reassess his future. His involvement in Nancy's copper scroll story and his ability to successfully fight for his life led him to explore a new career as a thriller novelist. Given all that he had seen and experienced, the challenge of composing a bestseller could be just around the corner.

Alan L. Moss is a unique and emerging voice in the thriller genre. His novels spin sophisticated tales of conspiracy, love, sex, and subterfuge.

Alan's writing draws upon Ph. D. research capabilities and many years in Washington, D.C. as a federal Chief Economist, Congressional Fellow, and Adjunct Instructor at area universities. In 2002 he put his government career aside and moved to the Jersey Shore to practice as an expert witness and pursue his writing. Recently, he and his wife of 54 years moved to Princeton to be closer to their children and grandchildren.

Alan has penned eight published books, six novels

and two nonfiction works. His novels often involve national and international issues and spectacular locations. After years of politics and bureaucracy, Alan has found the freedom of writing fiction an intoxicating and satisfying calling.

In his new novel, The Promise Of The Copper Scroll (World Castle Publishing 2024), three brave women pursue an ancient copper scroll despite terrorist violence surrounding it. A quake affecting a cave near the Dead Sea frees the scroll which finds its way to the research director of the Princeton Seminary. He believes the scroll may point the way to billions in gold, silver, and rare antiquities hidden from the Romans in 70 AD. When the Iranians learn of the scroll, they form a terrorist team to capture it and follow it to the treasure. Seeking the scroll becomes an unpredictable shell game with death and destruction facing each of the players.

Alan's previous work, The Choices: A Treasure Hunt Thriller (Cresting Wave Publishing 2021), begins sixty-six million years ago when a giant asteroid crashed into the Yucatan Peninsula, killing the dinosaurs and all other earthbound species. A graduate student in geology constructs a theory that the heat and pressure of the collision must have resulted in a treasure of unprecedented diamonds. A cast of fascinating characters race to obtain the stones in spite of deadly threats and an approaching hurricane.

The Samoa Seduction (October 2015 by A-Argus Books/W & B Publishers) is an eye opening thriller that combines the action of a drug company conspiracy, industry efforts to suppress wages, and government corruption with murder and a steamy affair. Settings include Samoa's lush scenery, the Central Canterbury Plains of New Zealand's south island, a resort on Hawaii's Molokai Island, the TranzAlpine Railroad, and tuna fishing vessels on the Tasman Sea.

Alan's earlier work on The Insidious Deception Saga chronicles how a pre-med student and brilliant college professor become entangled in conspiracies hatched by al Qaeda and a ruthless CEO. The two resulting novels include :Insidious Deception (Whiskey Creek Press 2013), and the sequel, Surviving the Endgame (Whiskey Creek Press 2014), in which a presidential election becomes a deadly contest between the international conspirators and those seeking their destruction. Rob Taylor, the series' protagonist, finds the love of his life and struggles to protect her from the conspiracy's violent tentacles.

Turning to Alan's nonfiction work, in May 2008 Praeger Publishing released Selling-Out America's Democracy. The book shows how special interests, through their lobbyists and the U.S. system of campaign financing, have denied a majority of the American population the policies they seek and have led the nation into a period of decline. The book includes telling interviews of Washington insiders and a four-part plan to restore the U.S. democracy.

Alan's initial published work is Employment Opportunity (Prentice Hall 2000). The book and its database provide an array of job search strategies and information that may lead readers to their career.
Alan is a member of the Authors Guild and International Thriller Writers.